He moved closer and drew her to him, kissing her with a thoroughness that took her breath away.

She closed her eyes and absorbed the sensation, feeling the tingling response of her lips and an answering heat that rippled through the length of her body. His hands moved over her, shaping her to him.

It felt unbelievably good, and she melted into his embrace, wanting the kiss to go on and on. It was madness, of course, but she had never known this deep-seated feeling of belonging in her life before, and it all seemed so right, so perfectly natural.

When he finally dragged his mouth from hers, she opened her eyes and stared up at him, startled, enchanted, tantalised and wanting more. But she said nothing, instead simply watched him, and wondered what could have drawn him to do that.

When **Joanna Neil** discovered Mills & Boon®, her life-long addiction to reading crystallised into an exciting new career writing Medical Romance™. Her characters are probably the outcome of her varied lifestyle, which includes working as a clerk, typist, nurse and infant teacher. She enjoys dressmaking and cooking at her Leicestershire home. Her family includes a husband, son and daughter, an exuberant yellow Labrador and two slightly crazed cockatiels. She currently works with a team of tutors at her local education centre to provide creative writing workshops for people interested in exploring their own writing ambitions.

Recent titles by the same author:

EMERGENCY AT THE ROYAL
IN HIS TENDER CARE
THE CONSULTANT'S SPECIAL
 RESCUE

THE EMERGENCY DOCTOR'S PROPOSAL

BY
JOANNA NEIL

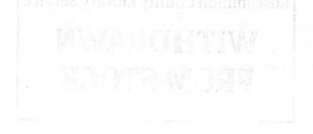

MILLS & BOON®

First published in Great Britain 2006
Large Print edition 2006
Harlequin Mills & Boon Limited,
Eton House, 18-24 Paradise Road,
Richmond, Surrey TW9 1SR

© Joanne Neil 2006

ISBN 0 263 18882 5

Set in Times Roman 17 on 20 pt.
17-0806-52095

Printed and bound in Great Britain
by Antony Rowe Ltd, Chippenham, Wiltshire

CHAPTER ONE

'Do you think you'll be all right here, Hannah?' Sarah asked, giving her sister a concerned look. 'I hate to leave you like this, but I have to go out to work. I'm on a special training week just now and it's not something that I can get out of easily.'

'I'll be fine. Don't worry about me.' Hannah's voice was low, her mouth a little stiff around the edges, as though it was taking a lot for her to keep going, and Sarah wished there was some way she could smooth things out for her.

'You could always ring Dad,' she suggested. 'He would probably be glad to help, and you know he dotes on Jamie. He thinks the world of his little grandson.'

'No. I can't do that.' Hannah shook her head,

an instinctive reaction, and the words came out quickly, running over themselves. 'Later, perhaps.' She composed herself and said more soberly, 'I need time to think, and Dad will only start asking questions, and he's bound to blame me for getting involved with Ryan in the first place. He'll start telling me that I acted foolishly, and I'm just not up to dealing with all that right now.'

Sarah grimaced. 'I think you're wrong,' she said with a faint lift of her shoulders, 'but it's up to you, of course. I'm sure that he only wants what's best for you, but in the end it has to be your decision.'

She frowned and looked around the small kitchen. Her cottage was cramped, short on space at the best of times, but they would make do somehow. At least there was a pocket-handkerchief-size garden where four-year-old Jamie could play in safety.

'You know that you and Jamie are welcome to stay here for as long as you need. Kingston, too.'

The yellow Labrador was asleep by the door,

his head on his paws, but now, at the mention of his name, he languidly raised a brow. He was frowning, as though the upheaval had been all too much for him, but after a moment or two, seeing that nothing untoward was happening, he sank back into oblivion.

'Thanks.' Hannah's features were strained. 'I'm sorry to put you through all this. I just didn't know what to do for the best. I was worried about Jamie. He's so young and he was getting upset at the thought of Ryan coming back and causing trouble. I know it was late, and I'm sorry for disturbing you when you were fast asleep, but you were the first person I thought of.'

'You did the right thing,' Sarah said in a soothing tone. 'You'll be safe here. Ryan doesn't know where I live—as I recall, he was away, working in Switzerland, when I bought the cottage—so he isn't likely to turn up on my doorstep.'

'I suppose that's true. I didn't really stop to think. I just felt that we had to get away. I knew that you would think of something, and that you would help me to sort things out.'

'I told you, anytime you need me, you only have to call and I'll do whatever I can to help. I'm your sister—I need to know that you're safe, and that Jamie is all right.' Her features softened. 'I'm just glad that he's sleeping peacefully now. It was upsetting for him, poor little mite.'

She had looked in on him just a short while ago, watching him while he slept, tucked up in her second bedroom, and she reflected on how angelic he looked, snuggled down under his duvet, his thumb in his mouth for comfort. 'He must have been worn out, poor thing.'

Just then, her mobile rang, interrupting their conversation, and Sarah found herself tensing instinctively. She glanced down at her watch and, seeing the time, it was simple enough to guess who the caller would be. Answering the insistent ring tone, she said her name briefly and then listened.

'Where are you, Sarah? I was expecting you

some ten minutes ago. You know that if you're not here when the first call comes in, we'll have to leave, don't you? We can't wait around for you.'

Mark Ballard's voice was gravelled, authoritative and threaded through with a hint of impatience. Sarah swallowed and said carefully, 'Yes, I know, I understand. I did try to ring you a while ago, but you weren't answering. I think your phone must have been switched off.'

'I was probably on my way to work.' He paused momentarily. 'Perhaps you should have left a message.'

'Yes, you're right.' She winced. Why was she always on the wrong foot in her dealings with Mark? Working with him didn't ever get any easier, did it? 'Look,' she murmured, 'I know that I'm later than we agreed, but it really couldn't be helped and I'm on my way. If I don't make it before you and the ambulance crew have to leave, I'll catch up with you at the first venue. I'll ring you to find out where that will be.'

'Do that,' he said. He didn't waste any time in small talk, but cut the line without further ado, and she stared down at her phone, feeling aggrieved and on edge. OK, so she was late. Wasn't she allowed any leeway? It was hardly as though she made a habit of it.

Hannah made a face. 'I'm sorry to be such a nuisance. Was that your boss? I know you said you were going out with the ambulance crew today. This is all my fault.'

Sarah glanced at her. 'Don't blame yourself. The crew isn't officially on duty for another twenty minutes, and the world isn't going to end because I'm not where I'm supposed to be. No one's that indispensable and, besides, the paramedics usually work alone. This time, because of the training commitment, they'll have two doctors going along with them.'

Even so, she was tense at the thought of letting Mark Ballard down. Theirs had been a strained working relationship from the beginning, and this could only serve to make life more difficult.

She slipped her phone into her bag and looked around for her medical case. She wanted to have it with her so that she could be sure she had everything she might need. Distractedly, she ran a hand through the mass of her unruly, honey-coloured curls.

'It's all part of a new hands-on initiative that Mark has thought up. He thinks it will keep us all on our toes, help us to communicate better with the paramedics and help us to understand the work they do. He's a great believer in team effort.'

She made a face. 'I suppose he's right, and it's good to get out of the unit and have a change of scene now and again. It's just that I don't feel that I'm quite up to par with what I'm doing in A and E just yet. I've been working there for a few months but I still feel as though I'm finding my feet.' She found her medical bag and started to drop items into it.

'I thought you were keen to work in Emergency?'

'I was, at first. It was what I aimed for when I went into medicine, and I thought it would be

a challenge. I wanted to see if I was up to it.'
She grimaced. 'Anyway, it's an essential part of
my training as a senior house officer.'

She was quiet for a moment, pushing a fresh
pack of latex gloves into her case, and then
added, 'I hoped that once I learned the ropes I
would be able to make a difference and that I
would at least have the satisfaction of knowing
that I was able to save lives, but I'm still unsure
of myself. Everything seems to happen in a
much more dramatic and immediate way in A
and E than in other forms of medicine.'

'It doesn't sound as though your boss is
much help. Does he know that you feel unsure
of yourself?'

Sarah shook her head. 'I don't think so, and
I don't want him to see that I'm uncertain. I
have the feeling that he had doubts about my
ability from the first, and I'm wary of adding
to that impression.'

'Why would he doubt you?' Hannah shot her
a quick glance. 'You haven't had any major
problems so far, have you?'

'No—well, nothing too serious, but, then, in the past I was always able to turn to Owen if I had any problems. Perhaps Mark thought that we were too close and that Owen was protecting me, covering for my mistakes.'

Hannah frowned. 'It would have been natural for Owen to do that, wouldn't it? After all, you and he were dating at one time, weren't you?' She was quiet for a moment, thinking things through. 'It must have been awkward for you when your boss took over from Owen. Isn't that why Owen left, because the two of them didn't get on?'

Sarah nodded, throwing some rolls of zinc oxide tape into the bag and adding fresh supplies of local anaesthetic. 'Yes, you're right.' She gave a small sigh. 'He didn't want to stay and be subordinate to Mark. As to Mark, I imagine he thought that Owen had been making allowances for me. He didn't seem to be very pleased to have me on his team, anyway.'

She made a face. 'I just feel, more than ever,

that I should be able to prove to him that I'm capable of becoming a skilled A and E doctor, but it's turning out to be much more difficult than I imagined.' Her blue eyes were troubled. 'I sometimes feel as though I'm completely out of my depth.'

Hannah frowned. 'Perhaps it takes some getting used to. There can't be many doctors who go in there and feel at home right away. There's a lot of responsibility, I imagine.'

'That's true. You have to think on your feet all the while and you have to make split-second decisions. I do my best, but I'm not convinced that I'm always up to it. I'm apprehensive, afraid that I'll do the wrong thing.'

She snapped the case shut and gave Hannah a brief smile. 'Anyway, enough of my problems. You should try to make yourself at home here. Help yourself to anything that you think you might need. There's plenty of food in the cupboards and the fridge to keep you going.'

She hesitated, looking around and wondering

if there was anything that she had forgotten. 'There are fresh towels in the airing cupboard, and if you need a change of clothes, you can take a look through my wardrobe. We're around the same size.' There hadn't been time to gather up very much from Hannah's place. Everything had been done in such a rush because her sister had been anxious to get away.

She glanced once more at Hannah. Her sister's features were pale, emphasised by the fairness of her hair that drifted wispily around her cheeks, and there were shadows under her eyes.

'If I were you, I would try to get some sleep. You had a disturbed night, and once Jamie wakes up you won't have the chance to get any rest.'

'You're probably right. I might go and lie down for a while.' Hannah made a face. 'I just feel so guilty for keeping you from your bed.'

'Don't be.' Sarah was already shrugging into her jacket and reaching for her medical bag. She went over to Hannah and gave her a hug.

'I have to go. I'll see you later. Give Jamie a kiss from me.'

Going out into the hall, she gathered up the morning post from the doormat. There was one letter, and she guessed from the handwriting that it was from Owen. She pushed it down into her jacket pocket before opening the front door and walking to her car.

Some minutes later Sarah manoeuvred her car into an empty parking space in the hospital grounds. Hastily, she climbed out of the driver's seat, locked up and hurried towards the ambulance bay. Was she too late? Would the crew already have gone out on a call? Her breath came in anxious spurts as she negotiated the internal road system and headed towards the meeting point.

As it happened, the crew was just preparing to leave, and the driver had already started up the engine. She broke into a run and was relieved when she saw Mark come around the side of the vehicle. He didn't look too pleased, but he said something to the driver, and then waved her around to the back of the ambulance.

'I'm glad you made it, but this is cutting it a bit fine, don't you think?' he said, his gaze narrowing on her. 'We were just about to go. We've had a callout to attend a boy who's fallen from halfway down a cliff.'

Sarah frowned, her blue eyes troubled. It was horrible to imagine what the boy was going through. 'I'm sorry. I'm just thankful that I managed to make it here before you left.'

She glanced at him as he pulled open the doors and ushered her inside. He was wearing dark grey trousers that fitted him to perfection, and a mid-blue shirt, crisply laundered and complemented by a subtly patterned tie. Long and lean, he was muscular, flat-stomached, and he managed to appear professional, alert and heart-wrenchingly good-looking all at the same time.

It wouldn't do her any good to dwell on that, though, would it? He was her boss, a consultant, whilst she was just a lowly junior doctor, and his opinion of her was probably at rock bottom. She looked away, concentrating her attention instead on climbing into the back of the vehicle.

'I have to say I don't think very much of last-minute efforts,' Mark said in a dry tone as he slid into a seat next to her. He was watching her, his grey eyes taking in her flustered appearance, missing nothing. 'I thought we had agreed that we would take some time to go over a few things before we started out today.'

'I know. I'm sorry.' She was battling with the seat belt, struggling to adjust it and strap herself in. Without a word, he reached over and completed the manoeuvre with slick, proficient ease, and she was mortified. She took in a few slow breaths to calm herself, aware the whole time of his cool scrutiny. It unnerved her. 'I came as soon as I could.' She looked up at him. 'How long will it take to get to where we're headed?'

'About ten minutes, but once we're there we have to negotiate a way down the cliff. There's no easy access to the beach and apparently the tide has cut off part of the bay.'

Sarah frowned. Did that mean the tide was encroaching on the boy? 'Who called the accident in? Is someone with the child?'

'A passer-by. He saw the boy from the clifftop and guessed that he'd taken a tumble. He's managed to make his way down to him apparently, and he's staying in touch with us over the radio. He said he's tried to contact the parents, too.'

'Do we know what the boy's injuries are?'

'The caller said his foot was at an odd angle. I suspect he's suffered a fracture.'

She nodded acknowledgement. 'Poor boy. I wonder what he was doing there? I'd have thought he would be in school at this time of day.'

'That's true enough, but from the sound of it he was perhaps being a bit of a daredevil on the way there, wanting to try things out. Climbing the cliffs is a dangerous thing to do at any time, but they can be especially tricky at this time of year. We've had quite a lot of rainfall lately, and now there are pockets of ice to make things worse. He was probably asking for trouble, but he's only eleven, so he can perhaps be excused for being young and foolhardy.'

'I suppose so.' Weariness overcame her and she struggled to suppress a yawn. She had been up half of the night, and now that the warmth of the ambulance enveloped her and the vibration of the engine was gently rocking her, lack of sleep was beginning to take its toll.

She was aware of Mark studying her once more. Perhaps he thought she was foolhardy, too. He didn't say anything, but she was conscious of his gaze travelling over her with slow deliberation. His expression was dark and brooding and for a moment she wished she could tell what he was thinking, but then she thought better of it. It wasn't likely to be anything good.

His nearness unnerved her. He seemed to exude energy and his whole demeanour was such a vibrant contrast to hers that it put her at a distinct disadvantage. She was far too conscious of him. His hair was dark, crisp and black, cut short in a style that attractively emphasised his angular, masculine features. His mouth was well shaped, forming now into an expression of probing curiosity.

'So, what happened? From the looks of you it must have been a memorable sort of night. What was it—a party? A new boyfriend?' His eyes darkened, as though he would see through her brittle shell to her innermost thoughts. Whatever her answer, she guessed that he wasn't going to be impressed.

'Nothing like that,' she muttered. 'Do you really think I would be so reckless, knowing that I had to come into work today?' He must have a very low opinion of her, if he thought that. 'Your problem is that you have no faith in me. Owen would never have asked me such a question.'

'Owen isn't in charge any more.'

'I know that.'

He sent her a long, thoughtful glance. 'Then perhaps you should get used to the idea.'

She frowned. She had spoken without thinking, and now she regretted bringing up

Owen's name. It was a constant source of friction between them. Ever since Mark had taken over as consultant in A and E there had been a barrier between them. He had always viewed her with a faintly sceptical eye.

'Perhaps you should learn to trust me a little more.' Perhaps he doubted her loyalty. It was common knowledge that Owen had wanted the job that Mark had won, and it must seem to Mark that she'd sided with Owen and resented his appointment.

She guessed that in the circumstances he wasn't going to warm to her easily. He and Owen had never really got on well together. The two men were equally well qualified, but in the end management had decided that Mark had the edge, and he was the one who had been promoted. It hadn't taken long after that for Owen to decide to leave the hospital and further his career elsewhere.

'What was the problem, then? What kept you?'

'I had to go and fetch my sister and her little boy from their home,' she said. 'The dog, too.'

He raised a dark brow. 'Why was that? More problems with her drunken boyfriend?'

Her eyes widened. 'You know about him?'

He nodded. 'I heard some talk. A couple of the nurses live near your sister and they've seen him in action. He was brought into A and E one night after a reckless binge, and they mentioned that they knew him.'

'Oh, I see.' Sarah felt awkward. It was one thing to have to work with Mark, but to have him know the unhappy intimacies of her family life was more than a little upsetting.

'So what happened?'

She swallowed. He wasn't going to let things go without some sort of explanation, was he? 'Hannah called me in the early hours of this morning. Apparently Ryan had turned up in the middle of the night, kicking the door and threatening to break it down if she didn't let him in. She didn't answer, and he went off eventually, but she wasn't sure that he wouldn't come back. He's done that before, and she was afraid of what might happen. I don't think he's ever been violent towards her or Jamie, but he has smashed things up before now. As it was, he damaged the lock and managed to splinter the wood.'

'Isn't it time that she finished with him altogether? From what I've heard, she'd have been wise to tell him that he outwore his welcome a long time ago.'

'I don't think it's as easy as that. After all, he is Jamie's father.'

'But they aren't married, are they? She must have realised that she'd made a mistake, from the very beginning.' He was frowning, as though he found the situation incomprehensible.

'People do,' Sarah muttered. She flicked a glance in his direction. 'Make mistakes, I mean.'

'So why didn't she cut her losses and move on? Theirs was never going to be a match made in heaven, was it? She must have given him some encouragement or he wouldn't keep coming back, would he?'

'I don't think it's as simple as that. It can't be, can it, when children are involved?' She was silent for a moment. 'Ryan isn't always bad, and there are times, when he isn't drinking, when he can seem like a regular kind of man. At least he's managed to hold a job down.' She winced. 'I suppose she hoped they would make a go of things, and in doing that she set herself up for being let down.'

Mark was staring at her with an expression of disbelief and she doubted that he would understand. This sort of thing could never happen to him. He didn't know the meaning of failure, did he?

She said carefully, 'You wouldn't know about these sorts of problems, would you? Your background is so different from mine. Everything in your life works in an orderly fashion, running smoothly like a well-tuned engine.'

'You sound very sure of that.'

She gave a half-smile. 'I am.' He came from a family where wealth and opportunity were the norm, where life was simply an ongoing, smooth path to success. His father was a prominent businessman who seemed to have the

Midas touch, and Mark seemed to have bene-fited from his parentage in every way. He was confident in everything that he did.

She stifled a sigh, wishing that the fog in her brain would clear. She was so tired, and yet she needed all her wits about her to cope with the challenges of her work. Without them she had to draw deeply on her inner reserves. A cup of coffee would be good right now.

'Are you going to be all right? Are you up to doing the job?'

She blinked. 'I'll be fine. It was a bad night, all in all, and I didn't get very much sleep, but you don't need to be concerned. I'll manage.'

'You need to be able to do more than manage,' he said briskly.

She didn't answer him. Instead, she closed her eyes and let the events of the night wash over her. She would be fine if he would just give her the chance to get herself together.

'We're here.' Mark's voice broke in, rousing her from slumber. 'Sarah, you need to wake up. I need you to be on your toes.'

She blinked once again, and looked around. The ambulance had stopped moving, and the paramedics were opening up the doors of the vehicle. Alarmed that she appeared to have dozed off, she struggled to get her brain back into gear. Reaching for her safety belt, she released the catch. She felt like death.

Getting to her feet, she moved along the ambulance and started to climb down onto the smooth surface of a standing area. Mark reached up to her, one hand grasping her elbow, the other going around her waist as he helped her down. It was a completely natural gesture on his part, an instinctive one, but even so it caused a ripple of heat to run through her, throwing her off balance momentarily as she absorbed the shock of his warm touch.

She laid a hand on his shoulder to steady herself and he looked at her, a glitter of something unreadable stirring in the depths of his grey eyes. Did he know the effect he had on her?

Probably not, she decided, getting herself

together. More likely, he was dismissing her as a feeble woman, made vulnerable through fatigue. Once she set foot on firm ground, he let her go.

Looking around, she saw that they were parked alongside a winding road that curved around the back of a cliff and led down towards the beach.

'The boy is down there. It looks like a fairly rugged descent, but we should be able to manage it from this angle.' Mark spoke to the paramedics for a moment or two and they began to prepare the equipment that they would need.

Mark turned back to Sarah, glancing down at her feet. 'It's a good thing you're wearing sensible shoes.'

'I wasn't sure what we would be up against.' A gust of wind blew errant curls across her cheek and she pushed them away with her fingers. Mark glanced at her shoulder-length curls and went on to focus on the rest of her slender figure.

Sarah tensed. Not knowing what to expect,

she had dressed in dark jeans that moulded themselves to her thighs, and a cotton top that clung to the contours of her chest, finishing off with a warm jacket, which was open at the front. She needed to be able to move freely, and this outfit seemed like the best option. Now she wondered if he would make some comment.

He didn't. Instead, he nodded briefly and appeared to approve of what he saw. Disconcerted, she looked at a point somewhere beyond his shoulder. His mouth made a crooked line, and he turned away.

She followed him down the rugged hillside, edging around to the foot of the cliff where their patient was lying. There was a small bay, with a stretch of dry sand, but the sea enclosed it, lapping at the foot of the headland on either side. Sarah could see why the boy had been tempted. This part of the Cornish coast was a wonderful location for aspiring rockclimbers, albeit that it was a forbidden pastime. It wasn't something that she had ever been tempted to try.

The boy was lying on the beach and he was clearly in agony. He was pale, with beads of perspiration breaking out on his forehead, and Sarah went over to him, filled with immediate compassion for his plight. She knelt down beside him, covering him lightly with a blanket, and spoke to him gently, trying to comfort him.

'He's in a lot of pain. I think he fell badly.' The man who had found him came to talk to Mark and the paramedics, filling them in on what had happened. He said his name was Andy.

He was a young man in his twenties, and he looked worried. 'I didn't know what to do for him. I was on my way to work when I saw him, and I think he must have been lying down here for some time. He had been trying to make his way up to the top apparently, but part of the cliff gave way, and he lost his grip. I haven't moved him. I was scared to death that he might have broken his neck, and I thought the best thing would be to try to keep him warm.'

'You did the right thing.' Mark reassured him, then went over to their patient and knelt down beside him. 'What's your name, lad?'

'Jacob,' the boy whispered. He tried to moisten his lips. 'It hurts. It feels really bad.' His mouth puckered and he said haltingly, 'I want my mum.'

'I think someone's gone to fetch her. She was at work, so it'll take her a few minutes to get here. It may be that she'll go straight to the hospital.' He added gently, 'Jacob, I'm Dr Ballard, and my colleague here is Dr Mitchell. We're going to try to make you more comfortable, but first I need to take a look at you, to see what the damage is. Can you tell me where it hurts?'

'My foot, my ankle,' Jacob managed, gritting his teeth against the pain. 'My mum's going to be mad with me, isn't she? I was on my way to school. I just wanted to do a bit of climbing.' The child was near tears and Sarah's heart went out to him.

'I'm sure she won't be angry,' she said. 'If anything, she'll be sorry that you're hurt.'

Mark said, 'OK. I'm just going to do a brief examination so that I can find out if you've suffered any other injuries.'

Sarah could see that there was a gross deformity of the ankle. Jacob had fallen awkwardly, and it was clear that he had dislocated the ankle and there was probably a fracture, too. He was lucky that he hadn't suffered any further mishap.

She glanced up at Mark and said softly, 'I'll get the syringe ready for the analgesia.'

Mark nodded. 'I'm worried about the length of time that he's been lying here. The circulation around the ankle is already very poor and I'm afraid that if we leave him any longer without trying to get the ankle back into its normal position, we're going to have major problems. There are deficits in his peripheral pulses, and I'm concerned about neurovascular injury.'

'You mean you want to try to reduce the ankle here?' She was worried about that. It would have been better to wait until they could get the boy to the hospital and into Theatre, but from the look of him, that wasn't going to be an option.

'I don't see that we have any choice,' Mark said, his expression grim. 'Let's get the analgesic into him and then we'll get on with it. The sooner, the better.'

He turned to Jacob and said quietly, 'We have to get your ankle back into the correct position in order to restore your blood supply, but we're going to give you a strong painkiller before we do that.'

Sarah gave Jacob the injection and they waited for it to take effect. Mark said, 'You might feel just a brief rise in discomfort as we correct your ankle, but then you should feel a lot better afterwards. Are you ready for us to do that?'

Jacob looked anxious, but after a while he nodded cautiously and Mark murmured, 'I'll need you to assist, Sarah. Will you hold him steady?'

Sarah did as he asked, while Mark gently grasped Jacob's heel with one hand and supported the patient's calf with the other. Then he pulled smoothly on the heel, and Jacob gave a sudden shout and sank back against Sarah's arm. Andy, the man who had stayed with him, winced.

'You were very brave, Jacob,' Sarah said. 'That's the worst over with now.'

Mark examined the boy's ankle once more. 'That looks much better,' he said.

'Yes, it does.' Sarah checked the pulses. 'That seems to have done the trick. The contours of the ankle are relatively normal now and the skin tension looks a lot easier.' She turned to look at Jacob. 'How do you feel?'

'Better,' he managed. 'It's still painful, but not as much.'

'We need to get you to hospital,' she told him. 'The ankle needs to be X-rayed, and I suspect that there is a bone fracture as well as a dislocation. We'll talk to the orthopaedic team, and they will look after you.'

'What will they do?' Jacob wanted to know.

'They will probably want to make sure that the broken bone is fixed into the right position, but before they do that they'll give you an anaesthetic, so that you'll be asleep and won't be able to feel any pain.'

He looked at her doubtfully. 'Are you sure?'

'I'm sure. You won't feel a thing, so you don't need to worry about that. When it's all done, they'll wrap your foot and your leg in a fibreglass slab so that the joint can't be moved and will have the chance to mend properly.'

Jacob seemed to accept what she said. 'In the meantime,' Mark murmured, addressing the paramedics, 'we need to immobilise the joint temporarily.'

The paramedic in charge nodded. 'As soon as we've done that, we'll move him up to the ambulance.'

As a team they made Jacob as comfortable as possible before they began the journey back up to the top. It was a difficult climb, hampered as they were by their load, but they made it without incident, to Sarah's relief.

She tried to stay on top of things as they set off towards the hospital. It was difficult with the drone of the engine once more lulling her to sleep, and she was fighting tiredness every step of the way, but she made herself stay alert for the sake of their patient. Besides, it wouldn't do to let Mark see her make another lapse.

Jacob's rescuer had followed in his car, and they met up with him at the hospital. 'Is it all right if I stay with him for a while?' he asked. 'I want to be here to tell his mother what happened. I phoned her and she said she was on her way.'

'Yes, of course,' Sarah murmured. 'I expect Jacob will be glad to have a friendly face close by.'

The orthopaedic team took over, and Sarah took advantage of the break in proceedings and went to grab a coffee. The paramedics were waiting around, enjoying a brief break before their next call, and she went to chat with them for a few moments. The coffee was hot and reviving, and she sipped at it gratefully.

As they waited for their next call to come in,

Sarah suddenly remembered the envelope that she had pushed into her pocket. She took it out, opening it up and scanning Owen's bold black handwriting.

'I miss you, Sarah,' he had written. 'I miss you every day and I wish you had agreed to come with me. You'd love it here, everything's so new and fresh, and the facilities in the hospital are second to none. The people are friendly, too, and you would have been in your element here. Won't you change your mind?'

She stared down at the page, her eyes becoming misty. She and Owen had dated for some time and they had been close, but when it had come to making a decision about whether to leave here and move some distance away, she had chosen to stay. Had she done the right thing?

'What's that you're reading?' Mark said, coming to stand alongside her. 'Anything that I should know about?' He glanced at the page and she folded it and pushed it back down into her pocket.

'It's nothing,' she said. 'Nothing to do with work, anyway.'

Mark's mouth crooked into a faintly mocking smile. 'Ah…a letter from Owen, is it? I thought I recognised that scrawl. How's he doing in his new job? Is he whipping everyone into shape?'

'He's doing fine,' she murmured. 'He doesn't have any regrets about leaving here.'

'But you wish that you had gone with him, don't you?' His expression was cynical. 'You haven't been yourself since he left. Perhaps you've come to regret staying behind?'

Sarah pulled in a long breath. Was she regretting it? She had spent some time mulling over her options, but in the end she had baulked at the idea of uprooting herself and going with Owen. She hadn't been sure enough of him or confident of his commitment towards her. Perhaps the truth was, her judgement wasn't good where men were concerned.

Instead, she had chosen to stay here and finish her posting in A and E, but she was beginning to have second thoughts about that. Was she cut out for it?

'Perhaps you're right,' she said. Mark didn't go out of his way to make things any easier for her. He was a difficult man to work with. He was constantly challenging her, demanding more than she had to give, and she struggled to keep up with his expectations.

His eyes narrowed on her. Already she was regretting that she had confided last night's troubles to him. It didn't help her situation for him to know that her family life was a mess.

Hannah was struggling because of her problems with Ryan and her efforts to bring up a child as a single mother, and in a way, because of that, her relationship with their father was guarded. Sarah's father didn't understand why Hannah couldn't find a more practical way out of her problems, and Sarah often felt like a go-between. It was wearing, constantly trying to keep the peace.

She shot a fleeting glance towards Mark. 'I probably made a mistake,' she said softly.

Mark's eyes narrowed. 'Even so, there's no going back yet awhile,' he said, his jaw flexing in a matter-of-fact way. 'You have to see your contract out.' He stared at her, his eyes dark and unfathomable.

Then he turned his head in acknowledgement as the paramedics' two-way radio crackled into action. 'Sounds as though we have another callout. We should go.'

Within moments they were on the move once more, and Sarah pushed her doubts and worries to the back of her mind. There was work to be done. Somehow or other she would prove to Mark that she was up to the task.

CHAPTER TWO

'KINGSTON, how could you?' Sarah gazed around at the scene of devastation that had once been her sitting room. 'What were you thinking of?'

The young Labrador stood in front of her, looking at her eagerly, the fabric remains of a cushion hanging from either side of his mouth. His tail wagged. He was clearly totally unaware that he had done anything wrong. This was fun after all…a new house, filled with lots of exciting opportunities to explore. What more could an overgrown puppy ask for?

Sarah looked at him sternly. 'You've been very naughty,' she admonished him. 'Look at the state of this place. A ripped-up cushion, newspapers shredded… And what's that? Were you just about to have a go at the rug as well?'

Shaking her head, she began to clear away the mess. 'I haven't time for this,' she said in a cross voice. 'I'm supposed to be going to work, not having to sort you out.'

It must have been beginning to dawn on Kingston that all was not well, and that Sarah was none too pleased with him, because he sat down and sent her a crestfallen stare.

'You can go and get in the car,' she said. 'I'm taking you to my dad's house. You can play in the dog pen there. You're not to be trusted anywhere else.'

She didn't think her father would mind. He had always kept dogs until a year or so back, when their family pet had passed on, and at least he would be around to take care of Kingston while she was at work.

The pen was at the back of the surgery where he lived and worked as a part-time GP, and it was big enough for the dog to exercise and sheltered enough to provide warmth and cover. There was an enclosed hut at the back of the pen, where Kingston could snuggle down in the old dog bed among some blankets. He would need it, given this bad spell of weather that they were having. It was late February, and there was ice around, black patches on the roads and the remains of frost on the roofs of the houses.

She arrived at her father's house some half an hour later. It was a neat, red-brick building, with a wide drive at the front and several large rooms to accommodate the surgery, a treatment room that doubled up as another surgery and a waiting room.

Her father's practice was a relatively small one, and with any luck he would be at home, nearing the end of morning surgery. He was lucky in that he had help with the practice. Now that he was close to retirement he shared the burden of looking after the health of the local community with another, younger doctor.

She found her father in his study, where he was working his way through a stack of patients' notes.

'Sarah,' he said. 'It's good to see you. What brings you here?'

'I have a bit of a problem,' she said. Quickly, she explained the situation. 'I daren't leave Kingston on his own in the house. He doesn't know the rules yet, and I'm likely to come back and find it wrecked. Do you think you could help me out?'

'Of course.'

Her father looked at Kingston assessingly as she trundled the dog around to the back of the house a short time later. 'He's a handful, that one, that's for sure.' His grey eyes were warm, though, and Sarah was glad that he had adjusted to the new arrival so calmly. He reached down and stroked the dog's silky head, petting him around the backs of his ears.

'Are you positive you don't mind having him here for a while? I couldn't leave him on his own, and I didn't know what else to do at short notice.'

'That's all right. I'll take him for a walk once afternoon surgery has finished. The exercise will do me good.' Her father was a fit man, trim for his age, and he still retained most of his light brown hair. He was strong-minded and personable, well liked by all his patients.

He looked at her thoughtfully. 'So what's happened to Hannah? Didn't she warn you that she was going to leave him with you?'

'She said she would only be gone for half an hour, while she dropped Jamie off at nursery school, but that was a couple of hours ago. I tried contacting her, but she isn't answering her phone.' She lifted her shoulders. 'You know Hannah. She probably met up with someone and forgot the time. Luckily, I'm on the late shift today, so I was able to wait around for a while. I can't delay any longer, though.'

'Just as long as it's not Ryan she's met up with. You'd have thought she would have come to her senses by now. As if it wasn't enough that she had to give up a good job when she became pregnant—now all she has is a part-time job that barely keeps her going.' Her father shook his head. 'He's going to be the ruin of her. How many times is she going to go through this?'

'I don't know.' Sarah sighed. 'He tried to get in touch with her yesterday, and she was trying to make up her mind whether she should ring him back.' She grimaced. 'I think she has too much on her mind just now. She's only been staying with me for a few days, but now that her door and lock have been fixed, she's thinking about going back home.'

'Would that be wise? I think she could do with some time and space to think things through, and it seems to me that Ryan needs to sort himself out once and for all.'

'She still cares for him, deep down. That's the trouble.' Sarah grimaced. 'I suppose she thinks that Jamie deserves to know his father, too. That's why she goes on hoping he'll change.'

Her father made a disgruntled sound. 'And pigs might fly.' He glanced her way. 'Are you off to work now?'

Sarah nodded. 'Yes, I should be on my way. Heaven knows what Mark will say if I'm late again. We're supposed to be having a staff meeting before we start work to discuss new procedures, so it won't be such a calamity if I'm not there for the start. Even so…'

'You had better get a move on.' Her father smiled at her. 'Don't worry about the dog. I'll take care of him.'

'Thanks, Dad.' She gave him a hug. 'I'll come and pick Kingston up as soon as my shift ends.'

The meeting hadn't started when she eventually arrived at the hospital, and people were standing around, talking. She was glad that she hadn't interrupted the proceedings. With any luck Mark wouldn't have spotted her slipping into the room.

She went and helped herself to a coffee from the filter machine by the window.

'I'm glad that you could join us,' a deep voice said. 'I was beginning to wonder if you were still having problems at home.'

Sarah almost choked on her coffee as Mark came to stand alongside her. She might have known that he wouldn't have missed anything. He used a dry tone, and she realised that he had guessed she had only made it by the skin of her teeth.

She gave him a brief smile. 'I'm hoping that they're sorted out for the time being,' she returned. 'I did my very best to be here on time. What's on the agenda for today?'

'Go and take a seat and you'll find out. We're just about to begin.'

She did as he'd suggested, sipping appreciatively at her coffee. Most of the meeting was taken up with a discussion of ways and means that they could use to improve throughput in the emergency room. There was obviously a need for change because patient numbers were rising steadily and the doctors and nurses were under pressure most of the time. It didn't help that they were short-staffed.

Mark had been brought in to the department to shake things up, and Sarah had no doubt that he would achieve his objective. He was energetic, on the ball, decisive, and she could see why management had chosen him instead of Owen.

Owen, on the other hand, was good at his job,

calm and tranquil, and far more easygoing. Those qualities didn't necessarily make for good management, though, and Mark certainly didn't suffer from any such handicap.

'Did you have anything to add to that, Sarah?'

She looked up as the sudden query caught her unawares, and she tried to collect her scattered thoughts. She stared at Mark. Was he talking to her? She had no idea what direction the discussion had taken. For some minutes her thoughts had drifted off, and now Mark was looking at her with laser-like interest, one dark brow raised in query.

He knew that she had not been listening. Drawing herself up in her chair, she said quietly, 'I'm not sure. Would you mind running that by me again?'

His mouth made a faint twist. 'Certainly. Dr Blake was suggesting that we could use a competitive system, with each doctor attempting to deal with as many cases as possible at each session. At the end of the month we could decide who was the overall winner and make that person A and E doctor of the month.'

Sarah swallowed. 'I don't think I could agree with that. Firstly, it does nothing to encourage the nurses, and could even alienate them, and, secondly, I don't think it would be a fair system.'

Mark was standing by a table at the far end of the room, and now he came around to the front of it and leaned back against the edge, his long legs thrust out before him. It was distracting, and she was far too aware of the strength of his taut thighs, firmly encased in beautifully tailored dark trousers.

He was studying her with a quizzical expression. 'Why do you think it wouldn't be fair? After all, this way everyone has an equal chance to compete. It would certainly help us to improve output.'

She glanced towards Dr Blake. He was young and lively, a senior house officer, on an equal footing with herself, and she recognised that he was very good at his job. He was clever, quick thinking and exceptionally skilled as a doctor.

He would have little trouble making swift decisions over the treatment of his patients, and she had no doubt that he could send them on their way, knowing that they had been given the care they needed. She felt totally inadequate alongside him.

'I agree with you that it would be a positive solution, and we would most likely see results if it was put into practice,' she said. She turned her gaze towards Mark. 'I just think that there would be too many problems if we do that. Who is to say that the doctor who treats the most patients has had a similar workload to anyone else? Some cases are more troublesome than others. It may take more time to deal with their particular problems, or it may be necessary to spend a while working out how best to help in particular circumstances.'

Mark was not impressed. 'Surely, over the course of the month, these inequalities would be evened out? Everyone has to take on cases with varying levels of difficulty.'

That might be true, but Sarah wasn't about to

back down. 'Maybe, but to go down this route would be to encourage snap decisions and speed for the sake of speed, and it could lead to carelessness. With all due respect to Dr Blake, I think it would be a bad idea.'

Shaun Blake frowned. He didn't look at all happy that she had disagreed with him.

Mark gave a faint grimace. 'Thank you for your observations,' he said. To Sarah's ears, it didn't sound as though he had appreciated them very much.

Addressing the meeting, he added, 'I'll take into account everything that has been said here today. I'm not going to make a decision here and now, but I'll let you know what course we'll be taking in a day or so.' He gave a brief smile. 'That's all for now. Thanks for your time, everyone, and now you're free to go.'

Sarah didn't move along with everyone else. She and Mark were scheduled to meet up with the ambulance crew once again and she was feeling faintly apprehensive about that. It hadn't been a good start to the day, one way and another. First the problem with Hannah not coming home, and now she had to contend with the fact that Mark was unimpressed by her participation in the meeting. She gave an inward sigh. There was nothing she could do about that.

'You don't appear to be too enthused about the day ahead,' Mark said, coming to stand beside her. 'Are you still uneasy about going along with the ambulance crew?'

She looked up at him. 'I don't recall saying that I was uneasy about it.'

'No, but I sense that you have reservations.'

'It isn't a problem,' she murmured.

He raised a dark brow. 'No? Then it must be something to do with the meeting that's troubling you. Am I right?'

'Not necessarily.' She pulled in a deep breath. If he would insist on goading her, then she would be straight with him. 'If I have a problem at all, it's with your management style. I don't go along with competitive practices or staff having to earn bonus points to score off one another. I prefer to work in an atmosphere of camaraderie, where everyone counts just as much as everyone else. I know that I haven't been here long, but I've been used to a more relaxed, inclusive style of leadership.'

'Like Owen's, you mean.' His mouth twisted. 'Sorry to disappoint you. I've been brought in to shake things up, and that's what I intend to do.'

'That's your prerogative.'

'I'm glad you realise it.' He gestured towards the exit door. 'Are you ready to go? We should leave now.'

'Yes, I'm ready.'

Their first callout was to a house where a woman had collapsed after suffering a suspected heart attack. They managed to relieve her pain and restore her circulation, and with any luck she would survive, given good care in the coronary unit.

Back in the ambulance, on their way to assist at another location, Mark leaned back in his seat and asked, 'What was the problem this morning when you first came in?'

She looked at him in surprise. 'What makes

you think there was a problem? I wasn't late. You hadn't started the meeting.'

'Maybe so, but I could tell from the way that you came into the room. You had that distracted look about you. I'm beginning to recognise it.'

She shot him a hooded glance. There was a wry look about his mouth, and she thought she detected a faint gleam in the depths of his grey eyes.

'I had to do something about Hannah's dog. He was on his way to tearing up my upholstery and generally wrecking the place, so I had to make sure that he was going to be looked after today.'

'Hannah wasn't there?'

'No. I've been trying to get in touch with her, but she just sent me a text message to say that she was sorry and something had come up.'

'Is she often unreliable like that?'

'Not usually. Sometimes she'll forget the time if she's caught up in something, but she doesn't go out of her way to let people down. I think she's unsure of herself at the moment. She has a lot on her mind, and she tries to fit things in between looking after Jamie and doing her part-time job.'

'What kind of work is she doing?'

'She's working in an office at the moment—not today, but for several hours a week. It's not what she's used to, but she did some secretarial training before she started work as a buyer for one of the big stores. She used to have a really good job and she used to travel, but all that's come to an end.'

'I suppose it would be difficult to cope with a job like that now that she has a child. It's one thing to travel and work long hours when you're footloose and fancy-free, but it's not as simple when you have dependants.'

She nodded. 'You're right.' She was pensive for a moment or two. 'That was how she met Ryan—she was working abroad, and he was out there doing some engineering work for his company. They were both staying in the same hotel.'

'Didn't you say that Ryan had managed to keep his job?'

'Yes, I did. I'm not sure for how much longer he can do that, though. He has a problem with drink, and it can't be helping.'

'It doesn't sound as though that's his only problem. There must be a reason for him to keep getting himself in the state he was in the other night.'

Sarah shrugged. 'I dare say, but I don't know what that is.'

The ambulance had now arrived at their destination, a factory where bottles were labelled and packaged, and the crew jumped out and went to attend to their patient. He was a young man who had trapped his hand in a roller mechanism. The fire brigade team was already there, attempting to free him.

'I don't think you've done any irreparable damage,' Mark said, examining the man's hand. 'It looks worse than it is, but we'll take you to hospital and get it X-rayed, just in case.'

Sarah felt sorry for the young man. He looked faint from shock, and although there was no dreadful damage he was suffering from severe bruising, and it would be a while before he would be able to use the hand again properly.

They waited at the hospital until their next call came through. 'We might as well grab some lunch while we have the chance,' Mark said.

'How can we do that?' Sarah asked. 'We could be called out at any moment.'

'I know that, but we'll get something to take out with us. Even if it's just a pack of sand- wiches and some coffee, it will keep us going.' He sent her a long look. 'I don't suppose you thought to bring anything with you, did you?'

Sarah shook her head. 'I did pack some lunch, but it's still sitting on the kitchen table at home. I forgot all about it when I saw what Kingston had done to my sitting room.' She flicked him a sideways glance. 'Anyway, you can hardly talk—I don't see you with a lunch pack.'

'That's because I was called away to help one of the junior doctors. I was on call at the hospital overnight, and I meant to drop by the café and pick up something, but I didn't get the chance.'

Her mouth curved. 'You mean you forgot.' She stared at him for a moment. 'Perhaps you're not infallible after all.'

His dark brows met. 'Did I say that I was?'

'That's the impression I had. I'm the one who suffers from constant lapses. You made that clear enough this morning.'

'I don't recall doing that.' There it was again, that quizzical expression, his head tilted a little, as though he had his doubts about her, as though he would like to find out exactly what it was that made her tick.

'Weren't you annoyed because I was almost late for the meeting? I thought you were scathing towards me when I disagreed with Dr Blake's suggestion. You might not like it, but I'm entitled to my opinion.'

His eyes glinted. 'I think you have the wrong impression of me. You were perfectly justified in saying what you thought.'

She sent him a narrowed glance. He wasn't saying that he agreed with her, but it was a concession of sorts.

They queued up in the café, and made their purchases. Sarah began to eat, savouring her hot Cornish pasty, and Mark was demolishing his sandwiches at a rate of knots. It wasn't long, though, before they were called back to the ambulance.

'It's a multiple road traffic accident,' the paramedic told them. 'There's been a pile-up at one of the accident black spots. Three cars were involved, from what we've heard. One driver hit a patch of ice and spun into the path of an oncoming vehicle. A car behind ran into both of them. There are multiple injuries.'

All thoughts of food were forgotten now. Sarah was keyed up, wondering what they were about to face. These kinds of accidents were serious. She had to be on the ball and decisions that she made could determine life or death. She hoped she was up to it.

Mark made a swift check of the casualties when they arrived at the scene of the accident. Another ambulance had gone along with them and the police were already there, setting up roadblocks. The paramedics went to attend to a woman and an older man, leaving Mark to tend the driver of the car involved in the initial skid. Sarah saw a woman, lying on the grass verge. She appeared to be conscious and a paramedic was by her side.

'There's a man in the other car suffering from breathing difficulties,' Mark told Sarah. 'He needs oxygen. He may have a pneumothorax.'

Sarah went to take care of her patient. He was in a bad way and one lung had collapsed, but she managed to inflate it once more, inserting a chest drain and taping it in place. 'How does that feel?' she asked. 'Do you feel more comfortable now?'

The man nodded. 'How is my wife? I tried to avoid the other two cars, but I lost control on the ice. I heard my wife scream.'

'One of the paramedics is attending to her. I'll find out for you.' The man's wife had been thrown from the car onto a grass verge, and Sarah guessed that she hadn't been wearing a safety belt. Her initial thought was that she might have escaped major injury when the car door had been flung open, but she couldn't be sure.

Sarah looked over to the verge. 'I can see her,' she told the man. 'She's sitting up and the paramedic is trying to put her arm in a sling. I don't think you need to worry too much.' It could be that the woman had sustained a fracture, but she was breathing and talking, and that was what mattered.

The man slumped back in his seat. 'Thank heaven,' he muttered.

'I need some help over here,' one of the paramedics called to her, and Sarah hurried towards the mangled car across the road.

'What is it?' She could see that the driver of the car had sustained a head injury. It didn't look too bad, but blood had poured down his face from his forehead.

'His condition didn't appear too bad at first,' the paramedic said, 'but now he's having difficulty breathing, and I'm wondering if the damage is worse than it looks. He has some cracked ribs, and it looks as though he has a penetrating chest wound, perhaps from some twisted metal.'

Sarah climbed into the passenger seat and looked at the injured man. 'I'm Dr Mitchell,' she said. 'Can you tell me your name?'

The man tried to turn his head. His lips moved, and she strained to hear his words. Looking at him closely, she suddenly began to feel very cold. Shivers ran down the length of her spine and she sucked in a shocked breath.

'Ryan?' she whispered. 'What happened? What are you doing here?' Another, more terrible thought occurred to her. 'Was Hannah with you?'

He made a faint nod. 'The paramedic...got her out.' He struggled to form the words. 'They...were worried...about fire.' The effort was too much for him and he closed his eyes.

Sarah guessed that they hadn't been able to move Ryan because of the mangled wreckage. He was partially trapped, although the firemen had managed to remove some of the metal that was confining him.

She looked around. Where was her sister?

Then she heard Ryan making rasping sounds and her attention swivelled back to him. She knew that she had to attend to him. His neck veins were distended, and she was worried that he, too, had suffered a collapsed lung.

As she worked to restore his breathing and to stem the flow of blood from his chest wound, she looked up and said urgently to the paramedic, 'My sister was with him in the car. Will you find her? Let me know what's happened to her?'

The paramedic nodded. He looked concerned, immediately on the alert. 'What's her name?'

'Hannah.'

He hurried away. It was all Sarah could do for the moment. She wanted to go and find her sister, but she had to take care of Ryan. It was her job, and she would be failing in her duty if she left him. She was torn. This couldn't be happening.

One of the ambulances started to move away. She heard it leave, and she wondered whether Hannah had been one of its passengers. The paramedic hadn't returned to give her any news.

Sarah managed to stabilise Ryan's condition, giving him oxygen and intravenous fluids, and after some time they were finally able to remove him from the car and carefully wheel him into the waiting ambulance.

Mark had finished working on his patient and now he called Sarah to join him.

'That's everyone accounted for,' he said. 'We need to get back to the hospital.' He studied her cautiously.

'But Hannah was here,' Sarah said in desperation. 'I need to find her. I don't know what has happened to her.'

'She's in the other ambulance,' Mark said. 'I spoke to her just a moment ago.'

Sarah clutched at his sleeve. 'How is she? What happened to her?'

'She's alive. She's conscious, but she's suffered an injury to her back, and we don't yet know how serious it is.'

Sarah felt dizzy all at once. 'Are you saying that she might have a spinal injury?'

He nodded, looking sombre. 'It's possible.

Without X-rays and MRI it's too soon to say anything more than that.'

Sarah felt the ground giving way beneath her feet. She began to sway and Mark quickly put his arms out to her and caught her in his arms. 'I've got you,' he said. 'Just take a moment. Don't imagine the worst. We're doing everything we can for her.'

'I know.' Sarah struggled to regain her balance and prayed for the world to right itself. After a while, she said, 'I'm all right. I need to go to her.'

'Good girl.' Mark turned her towards the ambulance and supported her as she stepped onto the ramp. 'In you go. Take a few deep breaths. I need you to try to hold it together. We have patients who need us.'

Sarah did as he said, pulling air into her lungs and making an effort to gather her thoughts. She had to be strong, for Hannah's sake.

Ryan was still conscious, but she was worried about his rapid breathing and the signs of respiratory distress, despite the attempts she had made to restore his lung function. There was a faint blueness around his mouth, and she was afraid that his condition was deteriorating. He was her patient and she was responsible for him.

They were still some way from the hospital when it became clear that something was badly wrong. Ryan's neck veins were distended, his blood pressure had lowered to a worrying level and his heart sounds were muffled.

She looked around to ask Mark for help, but his patient had suffered a relapse, too, and he had his hands full.

She was worried about Ryan's cardiac output. The ambulance started to pull into the hospital bay, and as the team came out to meet her she realised that the doctor with them was even more inexperienced than she was.

'I think he must be haemorrhaging into the pericardial sac,' she said. 'We need a thoracotomy tray.'

The doctor looked anxious, dithering as though he was unsure what to do.

Sarah said, 'Jonathan, he's bleeding into the

membranes surrounding his heart. If we don't do something about it, he's going to go into cardiac arrest.'

'I've never done a thoracotomy before.' The young doctor looked horrified.

Sarah guessed that the more experienced doctors were all busy working with patients. It was probable that the icy conditions on the roads had brought an overwhelming number of casualties into the hospital in the last hour or so and they were even more short-handed than usual.

'It's all right,' she said. 'I'll stay with him. Call for a cardiothoracic surgeon and arrange for a Theatre to be made ready. You had better order some blood for transfusion. Then come back because I'll need you to assist. We might not have time to wait.'

The doctor nodded. Sarah quickly donned gloves and a protective apron. She started to attempt aspiration of the pericardium, using a needle connected to a syringe and a three-way tap. If she could draw off some of the blood that was restricting the heart, she might be able to buy some time and improve the action of Ryan's heart.

It wasn't working. Despairing, Sarah debated what to do next. Ryan was getting oxygen via a tracheal tube, but all at once he wasn't breathing and she realised that he had gone into cardiac arrest.

She started to do external chest compressions, but that wasn't working either. The young doctor came back.

'The surgeon's busy with an emergency,' he said. 'What are we going to do?'

A nurse brought a thoracotomy tray, and Sarah stopped the chest compressions. 'I'll have to open his chest,' she said. 'It looks as though we're dealing with a cardiac tamponade. I don't have any other option.'

The young doctor looked panicked. 'Shouldn't you call Mark over?'

'He's working on another patient,' she said. 'I've already asked a nurse to call him in.'

She started her incision, and used rib retractors to enable her to open up Ryan's chest. Once she had gained access she attempted to evacuate the blood from the pericardial sac around the heart.

'Jonathan,' she said sharply to the young doctor, 'I need you to compress the aorta. I'm going to massage his heart.'

Using the flat of her hands, her fingers placed over the defects in Ryan's heart, she began the massage, willing life back into his body. It seemed hopeless, but she couldn't give up. This was Jamie's father, and how could she tell the little boy that she hadn't been able to save him? Whatever Ryan's faults, he loved the little boy, and when he was away from alcohol he could be gentle and kind, a different person.

The surgeon came at last. 'OK,' he said. 'What have we here?' He took in the situation at a glance and started to suture the defects in the myocardium. Once the sutures were in place, he said, 'We can stop the cardiac massage now. I'll check the cardiac rhythm and output.'

Exhausted from her efforts, Sarah stood back. She lifted her arm and wiped her damp brow with her elbow. She hoped that was the end of it, and that they had done everything that they needed to do to save Ryan's life, but the surgeon said, 'I'm going to have to shock the heart.'

The defibrillator was charged and he used the paddles internally on Ryan's heart. Sarah closed her eyes and prayed. None of this was real. It couldn't be real.

'I've found a pulse,' a nurse said.

'That's good.' There was relief all round. 'All right, I'm going to put in an arterial line and give him cefuroxime IV. We'll get him up to Theatre as soon as we can.'

Sarah was thankful to hand Ryan over to the surgeon. She had done everything she could think of and she was at a loss to know what more she could do. She said, 'He had a head injury, too. It didn't seem too severe, but I haven't been able to check up on that yet.'

'We'll do what we can for him,' the surgeon said.

Sarah pulled off her apron and gloves and tossed them into a bin. She started to walk away and the young doctor stopped her and said, 'Thank you for helping me out. You were terrific.'

Sarah didn't feel that way. She had worked on sheer instinct and necessity, and it wasn't over yet. Ryan's life was still in the balance, and she wasn't sure that she had done everything that she could for him. Part of her had been resenting the fact that he was keeping her from going to her sister. All the time that she had been working with Ryan she had been fearful for Hannah. What was happening to her? Why wasn't she able to do anything for her sister?

She went to find out where Hannah had been taken, and discovered that Mark was at her bedside.

'He took over your sister's care,' the nurse told her. 'He's been with her for the last half-hour.'

Sarah was glad of that. More than anyone,

she trusted Mark to do what was right for her sister.

He turned as she walked into the room. 'I've been monitoring her condition,' he said. 'I'm afraid she's in no shape to talk. We want to keep her as quiet and calm as we can, so she's been given medication. Your father's on his way.'

Sarah nodded acknowledgement and stared down at Hannah. She was being given oxygen via a tube in her throat and she was hooked up to an ECG machine. Monitors were bleeping, but her sister was very still, her eyes closed.

'How bad is it?' Sarah asked.

'She'll need surgery,' he said quietly. 'There's a spinal injury and we're uncertain yet whether we need to remove bone fragments or stabilise fractured vertebrae.'

'Is she going to walk again? Is her spinal cord intact?' She was shaking and hardly dared voice her anxieties, but she needed to know.

'I don't know the answer to that yet,' Mark said. His eyes were dark with sympathy, filled with compassion, and Sarah wanted to weep. How could this be happening to her bright, beautiful sister?

'What did the MRI show?' She paused, holding on to the metal bed head for support. 'You did do an MRI?'

'Yes, I did. It's hard to assess the level of damage at this stage. There's so much swelling and fluid accumulation. I've done a neurological examination, but that, too, is difficult to interpret. If the cord is intact, it may be that she'll recover some of her reflexes after the swelling has subsided.'

'What happens now?'

'I'm giving her steroid therapy, because that can help to improve function if it's given early on. In the meantime, we're waiting for the surgeon to come and take her up to Theatre.' He looked at her steadily. 'I'm so sorry, Sarah.'

His sympathy was her undoing. Her lips trembled and he hesitated for a fraction of a second and then came and put his arms around her, holding her close. She buried her cheek against his shoulder and sobbed into his shirt. He held her and comforted her, stroking his hand along her back, and she cried and wished that she would wake up and find that all this was just a bad dream.

It was only some time later when she realised that it had perhaps not been the most sensible thing to do, to allow herself to be comforted this way. Mark was her boss after all and, much as she might crave his support, she needed to learn to deal with her problems on her own. He wasn't going to be around to help her over every stumbling block, and showing him her vulnerable side had probably been unwise. He already had misgivings about her capabilities as a doctor. Wasn't she just giving him more ammunition to fire at her in the future?

She straightened up and carefully eased herself away from him. 'I'll be all right now,' she said huskily. 'I'm sorry if I've made a mess of your shirt.'

The fabric was damp with her tears, and he looked down at it and gave a slight shrug.

'Don't worry about it.' He looked uncomfortable, guarded, as though he, too, realised that their embrace had been a step too far.

He moved away from her, putting a little distance between them. 'I think you should go and talk to your father. He's in the waiting room.' He signalled a nurse to come and lead her away, and Sarah allowed herself to be ushered out of the room. She felt strangely isolated, as though she were utterly alone in the world.

CHAPTER THREE

SARAH watched her father as he pulled up a chair and sat down beside Hannah's hospital bed. He was shaky, unsure of himself, and it troubled her because she had never seen him this way before. He had always been a rock, steadfastly confident and reliable, but now he was a shadow of himself.

It was only natural that he should be this way. What had happened was distressing for all of them, terrifying in its aftermath, and she was finding it all too much to take in. How was she going to cope?

Mark was with them in the room, but he stood apart from them, talking quietly to a nurse. He had taken on the responsibility for Hannah's care, and deep down Sarah was glad of that. She saw that he was checking that everything possible was being done for her sister.

'We have to think about taking care of Jamie.' Her father interrupted her thoughts and she turned her head towards him once more. 'Will you go and collect him from nursery school?'

She didn't answer. She couldn't get her head around the fact that Jamie's world had been turned upside down, and now she simply stared at her father, not speaking, not moving.

Perhaps her stillness made him doubtful. He said softly, 'It might be better for him if you go, rather than me. He'll not think it unusual to have you go and meet him, since he's been living with you for a few days.'

'Yes, you're right.' She nodded, a faint, almost imperceptible movement of her head. 'I know I must go and fetch him. I just wanted to be with Hannah for as long as possible.'

'I understand.' He patted her hand, an abstracted, instinctive gesture. He looked devastated, as though his world had collapsed. 'I'll stay here with her in case she should wake up. I'll call you if there's any change.'

'Thanks.' Sarah pressed her lips together in an awkward movement. How on earth was she going to tell Jamie what had happened to his parents? Her eyes blurred with the sheen of tears. 'This is all a nightmare. I keep thinking that I'm going to wake up at any minute.'

'You're in shock,' her father said. 'We all are.'

She nodded bleakly and started to move away from the bed. Hannah was in the best of hands, she knew that, but it was a wrench to leave her all the same.

As for Ryan, he was in Intensive Care, still unresponsive after his surgery, and it weighed heavily on her that he might not pull through. She hadn't been skilled enough or quick-thinking enough as a doctor to ensure the outcome. The surgeon had done his best, but Ryan had slipped into a coma, and she couldn't help feeling that it was her fault. Was there something she had missed, something that she could have done to ensure his recovery? His head injury had seemed innocuous at the time, but the surgeon had removed a clot that had threatened his brain. Should she have acted sooner?

In a daze she started to move away from the bed. She needed to find her bag and her coat, but her brain didn't seem to be working properly and it felt as though a cold mist had infiltrated her mind and taken over.

She was aware of Mark speaking quietly to her father, explaining Hannah's condition to him and advising him of what was being done for her. Her father was a doctor, and he knew how bad the situation was, but even so it seemed to help him to have Mark carefully outline the steps that were being taken to look after his daughter.

After a moment or two Sarah started towards the door. Her steps were halting, as though her feet were unwilling to leave the room. Mark left her father's side and came over to her.

'I'll go with you,' he said, taking her by the arm.

'There's no need—' she started to say, but he took no notice of her objections.

'I don't think you're in any state to drive,' he said flatly. 'You're very pale and it's obvious that you've had a bad shock. I wouldn't feel that I was doing the right thing if I let you drive off on your own, especially given the bad condition of the roads. I'm off duty now, so it's no problem. I can take you home.'

Her senses were too numbed for her to be able to think clearly, but she managed to ask, 'What about my car? I'll need it for work.'

He held the door open for her and ushered her through into the corridor. 'You don't need to think about that now. You should take some time off so that you can be with your sister.'

'Thank you for that.' She frowned. 'But I'll need my car. I'll need to get back here.'

'I'll pick you up and bring you. Are you going to be staying at your father's house?'

She thought about that. 'I'm not sure,' she said at last. 'It could be unsettling for Jamie if we move him yet again, but it might be better for my father to have company for the next day or so.'

He nodded. 'I imagine that you'll all want to be together.'

They walked out of the hospital and a few minutes later they approached his car in the parking bay. It was a gleaming silver model, streamlined and expensive-looking, and she guessed that it reflected all the effort and ambition that had brought him to his position as consultant. It just went to confirm her view of him. They were worlds apart. She would never be in his league.

He helped her into the passenger seat and then went around to the driver's side and started up the engine. She leaned back, encouraged by the luxury of the upholstered interior and comforted by the cocoon of warmth and elegance that surrounded her.

She didn't speak. She was in denial, refusing to accept any of this. Words dried up in her throat and she felt as though she was choking on the sheer futility of what had happened. None of this was real. It wasn't possible that her life could change so much in the blink of an eye.

Mark's voice cut into the silence. 'Have you thought about what you're going to say to Jamie when you see him?' He sent her a sideways glance.

She shook her head. 'No. I don't know how I'm going to break it to him.' She pressed her lips together to stop them from trembling. 'How do you tell a child that his parents have been in an accident and they might not survive or that if they do, they might not be the same as they once were? I can't bring myself to do it. He's only four years old. He's too young to have to go through this.'

'You'll need to think it through, though, won't you?' he persisted. 'We'll be there soon. He'll be asking questions.'

Why was he provoking her this way, making her think of things she would rather push to one side? A hot tide of rebellion rose up in her. 'Do you think I don't know that?' The words came out more sharply than she had intended and she instantly regretted her tone, but she felt as though she was lacerated inside and every innocuous word became a criticism or a comment on her unworthiness, her helplessness. 'You have to understand…this has all happened so quickly. I'm still struggling to take it all in.' She didn't want to think. She wanted to let all of this pass over her as though she were caught up in a dream and in the morning none of it would matter.

'I know it must be hard for you,' he said, his grey eyes probing her face, 'but I think you need to prepare yourself. You need to start thinking about how you're going to tackle the problem. Jamie is very young, as you say, and he'll soon pick up on any nuances.'

He drew up outside the nursery-school building and Sarah sat for a moment, willing herself to move, to take those few steps that would take her to Jamie. Mark said nothing more, giving her time to get herself together, and after a while she released her seat belt and made to clamber out of the car.

'Do you want me to come with you?' he asked.

'No. Thank you, but he might be confused if you do that.'

She walked into the building and found Jamie getting himself ready to go home, shrugging into his coat and gathering up the pictures he wanted to take home to his mother.

'Nantie Sarah,' he said, his face lighting up as he saw her. He never could get his tongue around the word 'Auntie' and it had become his name for her, Nantie Sarah. She smiled at him.

'Where's Mummy?' he wanted to know. He looked around eagerly, frowning when he couldn't see her.

'She's…poorly,' Sarah told him. 'Mummy wanted to come and fetch you, but she's not very well. She has to stay in bed for a while.'

'Oh.' His lower lip pouted. 'Is it because of Daddy? Is that why she's poorly?'

Sarah stared at him, nonplussed for a moment or two. 'No, it isn't because of Daddy. What makes you think it was Daddy?'

Jamie shrugged. 'Daddy came to see Mummy at school this morning. Mummy was cross with him. She didn't want him to be here.' He looked at her, his blue-grey eyes wide and innocent. 'They were arguing. I 'spect she's got a headache now. She gets headaches a lot.'

Sarah guessed that Ryan must have persuaded Hannah to go with him that morning. Perhaps they had gone from the school to his house in order to talk things through. Then, when they had finished talking, he must have set out to bring her home. That would account for the direction in which they had been travelling when the accident had occurred.

She didn't think the accident had been Ryan's fault. Witnesses had said that it had been the icy conditions that had caused the cars to skid.

'Have you got everything you need to take home with you?' she asked Jamie as they prepared to leave.

He nodded. 'I want to show Mummy my work. We done numbers today. Look.' He waved a piece of paper under her nose, and she saw a series of coloured circles, squares and triangles, with numbers alongside. The teacher had drawn a smiley face on his work.

'That's very good,' she said, trying out a smile. 'You've been working hard, haven't you?' They walked outside, and she was aware that Mark had come to wait for them by the school gate.

She moistened her lips, all too conscious of him as she led Jamie over. 'Perhaps you can show Mummy your work another day. She isn't at home just now. She's had to go to the hospital so they can make her better.'

Jamie frowned. 'Is it the hospital where you work?'

'That's right.'

'Will you take me to see her?'

She nodded. 'Yes, of course I will…' She hesitated. 'But perhaps not today because Mummy needs to rest. She sends you lots of kisses.'

Jamie smiled. He put his hand to his mouth and made kissing noises and blew the kisses away with his mouth. 'That's what Mummy does when she's saying byebye.'

Sarah felt her eyes filling up with tears all over again. She blinked them away, and Mark stepped in and made his presence known.

'Hello,' he said, looking at Jamie. 'I've come to take you and your auntie home. I'm Mark. You must be Jamie, is that right?'

Jamie looked up at him, his head to one side as he studied Mark. 'Yes,' he said. 'Does my nantie know you?'

'Yes, she does. She works with me'

'At the hospital?'

'Yes, that's right.'

'Have you seen my mummy there? Nantie says she's poorly. I think she's got a headache,' he confided. 'She gets them when Daddy comes to see us.'

'Does she? I'm sorry to hear that.'

Jamie nodded solemnly. 'I wish Mummy and Daddy would live together, and then Mummy's head wouldn't hurt any more, would it?'

Sarah lightly tousled his fair hair. 'Perhaps not.' She sent him an affectionate look. 'Would you like to come with me to Grandad's house?

Kingston can play in the garden there, and it will be fun for him, won't it?'

Jamie nodded. 'Can we?' he asked eagerly.

'I'll phone Grandad and find out. He might say that we can stay over there tonight. We'll have to see.'

Jamie started to jump up and down in excitement. 'I like going to Grandad's house,' he confided in Mark. 'He's got a big, big garden. He's got lots of trees at the back, and I play hiding.'

'That sounds like fun.' Mark smiled at him and helped him into the car. 'We'd better sit you on a cushion and make sure that you're strapped in safely.'

Sarah was already making the call. She dialled the hospital's number and she asked a nurse to bring her father to the phone. Perhaps distracting Jamie this way was the best idea. He might be less aware that his mother wasn't around.

'What did he say?' Mark asked a minute or two later, glancing her way when she seated herself beside him in the front of the car.

'He thinks it's a good idea.' She paused and then added on a low note, 'He says there's been no change in Hannah's condition, or in Ryan's.'

'I doubt there will be for some time yet.' He started up the car. 'Do you need to pick a few things up from your house first?'

She nodded. 'Please. If you don't mind.'

He drove her there, and when they arrived at her street she pointed out the house to him and he drew the car to a halt by the pavement opposite her front door. Mark stepped out of the car and sent a quick glance over the cottage.

It fronted onto the street, but there was just enough room for a narrow border, and she had planted it with shrubs to provide colour all the year round. She had fixed up a trellis, too, and when spring came it would be bright with flowers.

She helped Jamie out of the car and once they were inside the house she sent him to play in the garden for a while.

'I don't think he'll come to any harm out

there,' she murmured. 'I'll just go and get a few bits together.'

'I'll keep an eye on him for you,' Mark said. He was looking around the small kitchen, and she wondered what he thought of her tiny cottage. It certainly wasn't what he was used to, she guessed, but at least the walls were painted a fresh sunshine yellow and she was pleased with the clean lines of her kitchen units.

She went upstairs and hurriedly pushed a few things into an overnight case, some clothes and toiletries for herself and the same for Jamie, and then she went into the living room and gathered up some of his favourite toys.

When she returned to the kitchen, Mark was at the sink, rinsing out a tumbler and a plate. 'I gave Jamie a drink of milk and a couple of biscuits,' he said, glancing her way. 'Are you all set?'

'Yes. I think so.' Looking around, she pulled in a quick breath. When she had left here that morning she had been exasperated, annoyed because Hannah appeared to have let her down.

Right now, she would give anything to have Hannah shrugging off her concerns, telling her that it had just been one of those things.

'Sarah?'

She looked up and saw that Mark was watching her closely. He seemed to understand what she was thinking.

'I'm all right,' she said, straightening. 'Perhaps we should go. Kingston will be pining for company by now.'

Mark drove them to her father's house. Kingston greeted them enthusiastically when Sarah brought him out from his pen, but he seemed to recognise that something was wrong. He followed them into the kitchen and sat down, watching them with a curious expression. Mark went over to him and stroked his silky ears. 'It's all right, lad,' he said. 'Good boy.'

Mark stayed long enough to make sure that there were no problems and that they didn't need anything more, but after a while he seemed to realise that Sarah wanted to be alone.

He said, 'I'll leave you to get settled.' He

glanced around. 'I expect you'll want to get yourself something to eat. You need to keep your strength up, and having some food inside you will help you to cope.' Perhaps he thought that she would forget the basic necessities of life. He looked at her carefully. 'I can come by tomorrow if you want a lift to the hospital.'

'Thanks. I'll ring you and let you know,' she murmured. 'My father might be able to take me there. I imagine he'll want to go and see Hannah again. He can probably get his partner to take over the practice for a while.'

Mark nodded. 'Are you sure there's nothing more I can do?'

'No, thank you. You've been a great help. We'll manage from here on.' She knew that she sounded cool and remote, and that was unforgivable after the way he had helped her, but she had no control over her emotions. She was numb inside, cold as though winter had lodged in her heart.

He left them, and Sarah set about preparing an evening meal. She didn't feel like eating, but

Jamie would be hungry and her father would need something to keep him going.

She put a casserole in the oven to cook, and then decided that she would take Kingston for a walk. Jamie would enjoy the exercise, and it would help to calm the dog down. She didn't want to think about anything else.

The next morning she dropped Jamie off at school and then went on to the hospital with her father. Her sister was awake now, but she was traumatised and weepy and she barely spoke, except to ask after Jamie.

'He's all right,' Sarah told her. 'We're taking care of him for you, and he sent you lots of kisses. As soon as you're feeling up to it, we'll bring him to see you.'

Hannah didn't answer, but closed her eyes briefly. Then, after a moment, she said, 'They won't let me see Ryan. What's happened to him?'

Sarah hesitated. She said slowly, 'He's in Intensive Care. They're doing everything they can for him.' She had checked up on his condition just a short while ago, but nothing had changed.

'But they won't let me see him.'

'Perhaps it was the wrong time when you asked. The doctors might have been working with him just then. It might be that they'll take you to see him later, when you're stronger.'

Her father said, 'Hannah, we just want you to concentrate on getting yourself well again.'

Sarah had no idea why the staff had stopped Hannah from seeing Ryan, and she doubted that the veto had come from Mark. It was most likely that the medical team thought she would be too upset and they wanted to keep her as calm as possible. They probably didn't want to take any risks.

She stayed with Hannah for some time, but it was clear that she was not in the best frame of mind to have visitors. A nurse came in and quietly asked them to leave. 'She's finding all this very difficult and she needs to rest. We'll stay in touch with you and let you know if there's any news.'

They said goodbye and walked out into the corridor. 'I think I'm going to go back to work,' her father said. 'I can't just sit around. It's soul-destroying.'

Sarah glanced at her watch. 'My shift starts in a few minutes. I think I might go and work, too. It will stop me from being able to think about other things, and at least I'll be close by if anything happens.'

'You'll phone me if you have any news, won't you?'

'Of course.'

Her father walked with her to A and E. He said, 'You know, we're going to have to do something about managing the situation with Jamie. With both of us working, it's going to take some careful planning.'

'I know. Between us, we should be able to work something out.'

They talked for a while, and when her father left, Sarah went to get ready for her shift.

Mark came over to her at the desk and frowned. He looked alert, efficient, totally in control, the opposite of what she was feeling. 'What are you doing here?' he said. 'I thought you were going to take some time off.'

Sarah shook her head. 'I want to be here, at the hospital. I need to keep busy, and if I'm working here I can drop in and see Hannah at any time.'

'I don't think you're ready to be at work. You're still in shock. You need to have your wits about you in A and E. I don't believe you're up to it.'

She stood her ground. 'I am. I want to get started.'

His eyes narrowed on her. 'What about Jamie? Who's going to look after him?'

She flicked a glance his way. 'I will, with my father's help. Jamie's at school for much of the day, and we'll work something out between us.'

'I think you're making a mistake. You're taking on too much.' Mark was frowning, his dark eyes searching her face. 'This is a difficult job at the best of times, and you can't do it properly if you've part of your mind on your sister and another part worrying about little Jamie. You said yourself that Hannah was sometimes exhausted, being a single mother, and here you are taking it on yourself to take up where she left off.'

'That's my choice,' she said. Her tone was decisive. It wasn't up for argument, and she wanted Mark to realise that. 'I don't see that I have any option. He's my nephew, my flesh and blood. I'm going to take care of him, and that's an end to it.'

'You realise that your sister might not be able to walk again? Are you going to take on his care for the foreseeable future?'

She looked at him directly. Did he have to remind her of that? As if she didn't know it well enough already. 'If it comes to that then, yes, I will.'

His lips firmed. 'I really don't think you've given yourself time to think this through.'

'I've made my decision,' she said. 'It isn't up for discussion. I'm going to take care of him.'

She picked up a chart and glanced at the

details on it. 'I'm going to find my first patient,' she said. 'Excuse me.'

He didn't argue with her, and Sarah tried to lose herself in her work. It was difficult because her mind kept straying to her sister and Jamie, and then to Ryan, and she had to keep making herself refocus.

Shaun Blake, the senior house officer who was on duty with her that day, came and found her when she was on a break. He said, 'I was sorry to hear about your sister and her boyfriend. I can't imagine what you're going through. If there's anything I can do to help, I hope you'll let me know.'

'Thanks, Shaun.' Her eyes misted over momentarily. 'You're right. It is hard to bear, but I've found that I'd rather keep busy than sit around waiting for something to change.'

She glanced at him. They had differences of opinion from time to time, but she respected him as a doctor and she said, 'I heard that you had landed a research post that starts once you've finished your stint here. I'm really glad for you.'

'Thanks.' He gave a fleeting smile. 'I hope I can make something of my sponsorship. We're looking into ways of treating coma patients, and I suppose that would be particularly relevant, given that your sister's boyfriend is in that situation right now. I wish there was more that we could do for him.'

She nodded. 'So do I.' She was pensive for a moment, then she added quietly, 'There was talk of celebrating your achievement. Some of the nurses mentioned a get-together of some sort.'

'Yes…In fact, it's all been arranged. I was a bit wary to begin with because Mark's father suggested that he should take over and organise the celebration, and I had my doubts about that. There's word going around that he had a hand in getting Mark the consultant post here.'

Sarah frowned. Whatever her own feelings were about Mark, she knew that he was a good doctor, and even if she wasn't entirely happy with his methods, he succeeded in making sure that the unit ran smoothly.

Shaun grimaced. 'I don't see it myself but people talk. Anyway, it turns out that Mark's father is holding a major fundraising event at his house, and he's asked us all to go along and lend our support. It's mainly so that he can raise funds for a new dialysis machine, but he's hoping to add to my sponsorship grant as well. It's too good an opportunity to miss.'

'You're probably right. From what I've heard, he has a lot of influence hereabouts.'

He glanced at her. 'I know that it's a bad time for you, but I'd be glad if you could come and join us. It would be good to have all my friends there. We're all signing up on the list on the noticeboard, so that he knows what number to cater for.'

'I'm not sure,' she said. 'I'll think about it… but I'm really pleased for you, Shaun.'

She went back to work, and after several hours on the go she was beginning to check her watch at intervals to see if she could make her escape and look in on Hannah.

A nurse said, 'Would you take a look at the

patient in treatment room four? He's complaining of pain in his throat, and he says his mouth is dry. I think he might have an infection, but I'd appreciate a second opinion.'

The nurse was a specialist, one who was able to deal with minor problems and prescribe antibiotics for simple infections, but she was clearly undecided how to proceed with this patient.

'Yes, that's all right, Megan, I'll take a look at him now.'

Sarah went and introduced herself to the patient, a young man in his mid-thirties, and he allowed her to examine him. He told her that the pain and discomfort had been coming on for some time.

'I hoped it would go away, but it's getting worse. Now I can hardly bear to eat, but I can't get an appointment with my doctor. The surgery's closed this afternoon.'

Sarah gently ran her fingers over the glands in his neck and looked carefully inside his mouth. She said, 'Martin, it certainly looks as though there's an infection of some kind, and I can give you antibiotics for that. It may be that a small, calcified stone has blocked the duct of your salivary gland and is perhaps obstructing the flow of saliva. That could explain why your mouth is so dry.'

He looked surprised. 'Can you do something about it?'

She nodded. 'It can be treated, yes. I'll need to refer you to an ENT surgeon, and he'll decide what has to be done. In the meantime, I'm going to send you to the X-ray department so that wc can get a picture of what's going on in the gland.'

'When will the surgeon be able to see me? I don't want to go on like this for long.'

Sarah made a face. 'There might be a bit of a delay. I'll mark your form as urgent, but you might have to wait a couple of weeks. There's a waiting list, I'm afraid.'

She glanced at him, seeing his disappointment. 'We'll try to make you more comfortable in the meantime. There are things we can prescribe that will help.'

She signed the X-ray form and sent him on his way. 'Come back to the desk when you've finished, and I'll let you know the results of the X-ray.'

Sarah watched him go, and went in search of another patient. She would put off going for a break until she had dealt with all the loose ends. That way, she could sit with Hannah for a while without worrying about being recalled.

The desk clerk caught up with her as she was writing up her patient's notes. 'There's a phone call for you,' he said.

Straight away, she was on the alert. Was there news about Hannah? Or had Ryan's condition changed?

It was neither. 'Owen,' she said, startled to hear his voice. 'I wasn't expecting to hear from you so soon.' She frowned. 'Did you get my letter?' She had only posted it to him yesterday, a quick note to say that her sister had been involved in an accident.

'I did. I'm so sorry to hear what's happened

to Hannah.' They talked for a while and she told him how things were and how they were waiting for news. 'It might not be as bad as you think,' he said. 'These things sometimes look worse than they really are. The tissues can take a while to heal.'

'I hope you're right.'

'You have to stay positive,' he said. On a lighter note he asked, 'How are you getting on in A and E? Are you managing to work things out with Mark? He was always a thorn in your side, wasn't he, checking on everything you do? Has he eased up any?'

'We get by,' she murmured. She felt uncomfortable talking about her boss, especially when he could appear at any moment. 'Have you managed to settle in all right at your hospital? You've been there for some time now, haven't you? Is the job turning out to be what you expected?'

'It's OK. I like it here and everything's running smoothly so far. Of course, it's not the challenge that it would have been there.' He was silent for a moment. 'I feel cheated about that. I still feel that the job should have been mine.'

'I know how much you wanted it.'

'I was well enough qualified and I'd been running the show for a while. I could have easily made the grade, but it's not what you know, it's who you know, isn't it? I'm sure Mark only got to be consultant because his father made a huge donation to the new renal unit.'

Sarah pulled in a quick breath. 'What makes you think that?'

'It's common knowledge. His father's as rich as Croesus and he knew that Mark wanted the job. He couldn't have found a better way of making sure that he got it.'

She frowned. 'Rich father or not, things can't be that simple, surely?'

Owen laughed. 'Don't you believe it. Money can make anything happen.'

A nurse stopped by the desk and signalled that a patient was waiting, and Sarah nodded acknowledgement. She half turned and saw that Mark had come to stand just a short distance away from her. Horrified, she wondered how much he had heard of their conversation.

She said, 'Owen, I have to go. I have patients waiting. I'll talk to you again, soon.'

She put the receiver down and was unhappy to see that her hand was shaking. There couldn't be any truth in what Owen had said, could there? Much as she was cautious around Mark, she had always believed that he was an excellent doctor and that he had worked hard for his success. Now Owen had put doubts in her mind.

Mark directed a glance her way. 'Is something bothering you?' he asked. 'I gather that was Owen that you were talking to. Has he said something to give you pause for thought?'

She knew then that he must have heard what Owen had said. His expression said it all.

'No,' she said. 'He was just asking after Hannah.'

His mouth made an odd shape. It was obvious that he didn't believe her, but he said nothing more on the subject. Instead, he signed off a chart and turned towards her.

'I've been looking through your patient files,' he said. 'Megan told me that you were ready to discharge a patient who has a salivary gland problem?'

She nodded. 'That's right. I passed the chart to you for your signature.' She frowned. 'Is something wrong?'

'I think there may be.' His expression was grim. 'I saw the X-ray and I decided that I should take a look at him. I don't think we should be discharging him just yet.'

Sarah was startled. 'Why not? Did I miss something?'

'I believe you might have. I suspect your patient has a tumour, and I'd prefer to have a surgeon look at it right away. It may be that it's benign at the moment, but these things can turn malignant, and I don't want to waste any time getting him treated.'

Her jaw dropped. 'But it looked like a simple case of a stone in the duct and a superimposed infection. How could I have got it so wrong? Surely he's too young to have a tumour in the submandibular gland?'

'They're rare, I grant you, but I'm suspicious about this one. I'd prefer to err on the side of caution, and I want him to see a surgeon today.'

Sarah was devastated. 'I thought I had done the right thing.' She went and checked the X-ray once more, trying to discover where she had gone wrong. It made her feel wretched to know that she might have missed something serious.

'You're tired and overwrought,' Mark said, 'and when you're in that state of mind it's easy to miss something. As it is, tumours such as these are not easy to spot, so we should do an ultrasound scan to check.'

'I'll go and organise it.' She started to turn away, her mind reeling.

He put a hand out to stop her. 'There's no need. I've already done that. You should go and take a break. Go home. I'll take over from here.'

She stared at him, anguished by her mistake. 'But I…I have to put this right.'

'You don't. I told you that you shouldn't be here today. You're not ready to be at work. As to this patient, you had set things in motion for him to see a specialist, so nothing bad would have come of it. It's just that I think it's best for him to be treated right away.'

Sarah nodded. 'Yes, of course.' She stared up at him in despair, floundering, like a fish out of water. He believed that she had made yet another mistake and he wasn't giving her the chance to put it right. She couldn't make sense of what was happening to her. How many more things could go wrong?

CHAPTER FOUR

'NO, YOU can't have it. Let go.' Jamie's voice sounded an alarm bell in Sarah's head, and she hurried into the living room to check what was going on.

'Kingston, drop it,' Jamie shouted. He was chasing the dog around the room, but stopped as soon as he saw Sarah. He waved his arms in a gesture of astonishment. 'He keeps trying to run off with my toys,' he exclaimed.

The evidence was still in Kingston's mouth, and Sarah grabbed the dog's collar and removed the prized possession. 'You can't have Jamie's truck,' she told him sternly. 'Go and play with your ball instead.'

Kingston's ears perked up. Ball? That seemed to jog a distant memory. He'd heard that before, somewhere or other... Ball... He knew ball. Looking around, he went to sniff it out.

Sarah glanced at Jamie. 'We have to go soon, chick. Will you put your toys away for me, please? Then we'll get in the car and go with Grandad to see your mummy.'

Jamie gave a whoop of joy. 'Yes,' he shouted. 'Yes...I want to see Mummy.'

He looked at her eagerly, and Sarah wished that she could be as positive about the meeting as he was. 'You know that she won't be able to sit up to talk to you, don't you...and that we can only visit for a little while? The nurse said we could have ten minutes. That's not very long.'

The nursing staff were worried that a longer visit would result in both mother and son being upset and they were wary of Hannah's spine being further damaged if she tried to get closer to her little boy.

He nodded. 'I'm going to give her my flowers. She'll like those.'

'Yes, she will.'

Sarah turned away, not wanting Jamie to

see her expression. Her eyes filled up with tears whenever she thought of her sister lying in the hospital bed, unable to move. It was heartbreaking.

Jamie was full of anticipation, though, and some time later they went to the hospital and headed for Hannah's room. Jamie went over to his mother's bedside.

'See what I brought you?' he said eagerly, thrusting the posy of flowers forward.

'They are beautiful,' Hannah said softly. 'Come here and give me a kiss.'

Jamie pressed a kiss on his mother's cheek and talked to her for a while, telling her about his friends and everything that was going on at school. Hannah listened and put in a comment every now and again. She was trying very hard to put on a cheerful face for her young son, and Sarah could only guess at how difficult that must be for her.

Sarah's father was sitting beside the bed, and now he leaned forward and spoke quietly to Hannah. 'Are you bearing up all right? Is there anything we can bring in for you? Some books on audiotape, perhaps?'

'That would be good, thanks.' Hannah was doing her best to be amenable, but the light had gone out of her eyes and Sarah felt wretched for her.

It was a wrench when she had to take Jamie out of the room a short time later, but the nurse told him, 'When your mummy is feeling a little bit better, she'll be able to sit in a chair and talk to you, and then you can stay for a little bit longer. Will you like that?'

Jamie nodded solemnly. He looked up at Sarah. 'Is she going to be better soon?'

'I hope so, Jamie.'

She walked with him along the corridor, showing him the hospital gardens from the windows, doing what she could to take his mind off having to leave his mother. Her father was going to stay with Hannah for a little while longer, and more than anything, Sarah hoped that he would be able to bring her out of her depression.

She was pointing out to Jamie the fountain and a collection of four bronze statues that decorated a paved area outside the building when she glanced around and saw that Mark was coming their way. His stride was long and purposeful, and he looked good, wearing a beautifully tailored suit that sat easily on his masculine frame, so that her heart made a strange little lurch in her chest.

'I thought you might be around here,' he said. He glanced at Jamie. 'Have you been to see your mummy?'

Jamie nodded.

He must have sensed Jamie's reservations, because he murmured, 'I expect that you'll be able to see her again very soon.' He looked fleetingly at Sarah. 'What are you going to do now? Are you on your way to the café?'

'I thought we might go and get a snack while we wait for my dad,' she said. 'I promised Jamie that he could choose what he wanted.'

'Would you mind if I come along with you?

I'm on a break and I was hoping that we might be able to have a quick chat.'

She was surprised, but she murmured, 'That's all right, of course you can come with us.' She had no idea what it was that he wanted to talk to her about. Had she done something wrong? Had one of her patients suffered a relapse?

'That's good.' He looked down at Jamie, and walked along with them, talking to the little boy and gently getting him to open up to him.

Jamie was solemn at first, but gradually he began to lose his shyness, and Sarah sensed that there was a rapport between the two of them. Mark seemed to know how to bring out the best in Jamie, and soon the little boy was chuckling and telling Mark how he sometimes wrestled with Kingston.

'He keeps rolling over on his back, and he likes his tummy tickled,' he confided, 'and sometimes he puts his paw up to me and we shake hands.' His voice was gleeful.

Sarah was glad that Jamie was happy once more. They went into the hospital café and loaded their trays. Jamie chose milk and cake, and Sarah settled for coffee. Mark added a pack of sandwiches and bought a small puzzle box from a collection of toys that were in a basket on the counter. He gave the box to Jamie.

'Have you played with one of those before?'

The little boy inspected it carefully and shook his head.

'I'll start you off, then,' Mark said. He showed Jamie how to manoeuvre the pieces, and then said, 'Do you think you can manage it by yourself now?'

Jamie nodded, smiling. 'Thanks,' he said, looking up at him with wide eyes. He took the puzzle over to their table and immediately became absorbed in working out how to fit all the pieces together and push them into the right places.

'You said that you wanted to talk to me,' Sarah murmured, glancing at Mark when they had seated themselves. 'Is it about work?' She was concerned. 'Have there been any repercussions over the man with the tumour?'

He shook his head. 'No, that's all been dealt with satisfactorily. The surgeon removed the growth, and we were lucky in that it was benign. We caught it in time.'

'I'm glad.' She gave a relieved sigh and stirred her coffee absently. Would it have made a difference if he had been discharged and left to wait for an appointment? Who could tell? It was only because of Mark's vigilance that the man had received prompt treatment. She said cautiously, 'What was it that you wanted to talk to me about?'

'It's to do with the fundraising dinner tomorrow evening. I noticed that your name wasn't on the list, and I know that this is a bad time for you, but I think it would be good for you if you could manage to come along.'

She had tried not to think about the dinner. She had enough things on her mind already, and anyway, after what Owen had said about Mark's father and his influence in getting his son the job in A and E, she had thought it better to steer clear. She didn't want to be drawn into any gossip that might start up, and how could she avoid that if the function was being held at his father's house? Perhaps Mark's father didn't care one way or the other if his motives were questioned.

'I don't think I can bring myself to sign up for anything right now,' she said. 'I'm worried about Hannah and Ryan, and there's Jamie to look after. I don't want to have to think about anything else at the moment.'

'I realise that.' He looked at her carefully. 'I know what you're going through, but I think it would do you good in a lot of ways to come along. I think you'll feel better for a change of scene, and it isn't just a commonplace get-together—we do this once a year, and it's a highlight, an out-of-the-ordinary occasion. This time it's extra-special because we're also celebrating Shaun Blake's promotion. He's been given sponsorship and offered the chance to do research when his stint as senior house officer comes to an end.'

'Yes, I heard about that. I'm pleased for him,

and I know the fundraising effort is for a good cause—a new dialysis machine—but I just don't feel up to joining in any social events right now. I don't think I would be very good company for anyone at the moment.'

Jamie interrupted them, waving his puzzle in front of her nose to show her how it was coming along. 'I done that bit, see?' he said.

'You're doing very well,' Sarah acknowledged. 'Where does that piece go? Does it fit in there?' She pointed to one of the coloured sections, and Jamie studied it once more.

'You don't need to put yourself out to be good company,' Mark said. 'Just being there would be enough.'

She frowned. 'It isn't as simple as that, though, is it? I expect there will be a lot of wealthy people there, people who have a lot of clout, and I don't feel that I belong. I don't think I can add anything, and I'm not up to mixing with management chiefs and administrators and so on at the moment.'

Mark said, 'Sarah, you shouldn't worry about

having to fit in. You're not going to stand out from the crowd. Everyone from A and E who isn't on duty will be there to support Shaun. There aren't many occasions when we can socialise outside work, but this is a one-off and it's a chance for us all to get to know each other better. I'd really appreciate it if you would try to be there.'

He wasn't saying that anyone would be put out if she didn't attend, but she wondered if Shaun would take offence. He had been all right with her the last time they had spoken, but he hadn't liked it when she had disagreed with his suggestion about introducing a competitive element in A and E. There was a faint possibility that he might take it as a slight if she didn't publicly acknowledge his success by attending the dinner.

She said thoughtfully, 'I suppose I really should show Shaun some support. He's a good doctor, and I'm pleased for him. I know he's always wanted to do research alongside his work in A and E. I think he'll go far.'

'So do I.' He gazed at her searchingly. 'Does that mean that you'll come along?'

'I'll think about it,' she conceded. 'A lot will depend on whether or not my father agrees to look after Jamie.'

'I could come and pick you up. Shall we say seven-thirty tomorrow evening?'

He wasn't taking a chance that she might try to slide out of it, was he? She made a faint grimace. 'I'll let you know.'

They finished their coffee, and Mark glanced down at his watch. 'I should be getting back to work. We've been really busy today.'

A short time later they parted company, and Sarah and Jamie headed back towards Hannah's room.

She told her father about the dinner that evening when they were having supper at his house. They had decided that it was easier for them all to live with him for a while, and Sarah could relax, knowing that Kingston could safely be left in the daytime.

'I don't feel right about going out while Hannah and Ryan are so ill. I think that Mark realises that I probably won't be going.'

'I think you should go with him,' her father said. 'I'm happy to look after Jamie. I'm not on call tomorrow evening.'

She looked at him in surprise. 'I didn't expect you to say that. I thought you would agree with me.'

He shook his head. 'I think it's a good idea for you to go. There's nothing you can do to help Hannah except to take care of Jamie and try to keep her spirits up, and there isn't going to be any change in her condition for a while yet. As for Ryan, his coma hasn't lessened, and it won't do any of us any good to sit around moping.'

With even her father on Mark's side, Sarah couldn't see any way of getting out of it. Did she have any choice? She didn't want to be seen as having a sour-grapes attitude.

When Mark rang to find out what she had decided, she reluctantly told him that she would go with him.

'I'm glad,' he said.

The next evening she was out of sorts, along with the weather, which seemed to be doing its best to emulate her mood. There had been no good news from the hospital, and now the heavens had opened once more and she could hear the relentless beat of raindrops against her window.

She tried to ignore it and did her best to make herself look as presentable as possible. It was going to be a formal occasion so she picked out a simple, classic evening dress from her wardrobe, laying it out on the bed while she showered. She washed and dried her hair, teasing her riotous curls into an attractive style and securing them here and there with small diamanté clips.

The dress was pale blue, with delicate shoulder straps, and shot through with lustrous threads. It clung where it touched, emphasising the shapeliness of her feminine curves a little more than she felt comfortable with. It was the only dress she possessed that would do for an occasion like this, though, so she smoothed it down and then slid her feet into stiletto-heeled shoes.

'Do I look all right?' she asked her father worriedly, when she was finally ready. 'Will I do?'

'You look lovely,' he said.

Relieved, she told him, 'Jamie's already fast asleep, so you shouldn't have any trouble there. I've just been in and tucked him up, and Kingston is guarding the landing outside his door.'

Her father smiled. 'You go off and try to have a good time. We'll be fine.'

The doorbell rang just a moment later, and when she opened the door Mark was waiting for her. He was dressed in an immaculate black evening suit that screamed expensive tailoring, and there was a spattering of raindrops across the shoulders of his jacket.

'Do you want to come in out of the rain?' she asked.

He didn't answer but simply stared at her, his glance shifting from the top of her head to her feet and back up again.

'Is something wrong?' she asked, suddenly

doubtful once more. 'I wasn't sure what to wear, but I know these occasions are formal. Should I go and change into something else?'

'No way,' he said, coming out of his reverie and looking her over with marked interest. 'You look fabulous.' He was still staring at her as though he couldn't believe his eyes. 'You take my breath away.'

Was it true? A faint wave of heat ran through her cheeks, and she glanced at him fleetingly, not knowing how to respond. 'Just come in for a moment and I'll go and get my bag,' she muttered. 'Perhaps you can say hello to my father.'

The two men talked for a while, and then Mark glanced at his watch. 'We should be getting on our way,' he murmured. 'Dinner's at eight-fifteen and I need to be there on time to help my parents greet their guests.' He gave a brief smile. 'Some very influential people are going to be there this evening.'

Her father smiled. 'I hope you raise lots of money,' he said.

Mark's parents lived in an exclusive area in the outer region of the town. It wasn't too far away, though, just a short drive, a journey of some fifteen minutes or so, and it wasn't long before they reached their destination. Mark parked the car on the gravelled forecourt in front of the house, and they ran towards the covered porch to escape the rain. It was a palatial residence, set in its own grounds that spread for some distance all around.

Offering her the support of his arm, Mark escorted her through the main doors and inside to the large hallway.

Doors led from off in various directions, and she saw that the main event was going on in a large room to the left. It looked like a ballroom, grand in size, and from where she stood she could see the glitter of chandeliers. Music was playing, and she could hear the chatter of voices.

'Let's go and find the others,' Mark said. They walked through double doors into the room where most of their colleagues from A and E were already gathered at the far end.

Tables were set out at one side of the room, where they would dine.

They went over to greet their colleagues and Mark handed her a glass of wine, lifted from the tray of a passing waiter. She sipped at it.

They talked as a group for a while, and then Mark said, 'I must go and circulate and say hello to some of the other guests. Will you be all right if I leave you for a time?'

'Yes, of course.' She hadn't really expected him to stay with her for the evening, but now it occurred to her that she might be able to slip away early if he was going to be occupied elsewhere. She finished her drink and put the glass down on a table.

Shaun was at the centre of the gathering, and when he had finished talking to his companion Sarah said, 'Congratulations once again, Shaun. I'm happy for you that you've landed the research post. You must be very pleased about it. It's what you've wanted for a long time, isn't it?'

He nodded. 'It's true. It's something I set my

sights on, and fortunately I've been granted enough money to carry out my research for a whole year.'

'I'm glad that it's all worked out for you.' She smiled at him. Mark had disappeared into the crowd, and as a waiter came by and offered a tray of drinks, Shaun took two glasses, handing one to Sarah.

'Thank you.' She sipped the champagne, crinkling her nose as the bubbles fizzed on her tongue and effervesced at the back of her throat.

'Don't you like it?' Shaun asked.

'I love it.' She laughed. 'I'm just not used to it.'

At dinner, Mark was seated next to her, and on his other side was a woman he introduced as a business associate of his father. He talked to both of them, and when the woman enquired about the dialysis machine, he outlined the venture and added encouragement to his father's fundraising efforts. Sarah spoke to Shaun on her left, but she couldn't help feeling a little lost and out of place. What was she doing here amongst all these wealthy people when her sister was lying in a hospital bed, unable to walk?

She ate her meal, sampling the delicious food and savouring it slowly. Afterwards the band took up position on a dais at the far end of the room and soon music filled the air.

Mark took her to one side and talked to her for a while, until his mother came and took him away to meet someone. His mother was an attractive woman, friendly and lively, anxious to make sure that the evening went well.

People began to take to the dance floor. Sarah talked to Megan, struggling to hear what she was saying over the sound of a fast dance number. After a few minutes, when Sarah glanced around, she saw that Mark was on the dance floor, moving to the beat with one of the guests, a slender girl with flowing black hair.

She turned back to her friends and tried not to mind. Why should it bother her if he was enjoying himself with an attractive young woman?

She tried to put him from her mind and made an effort to join in the general chatter. From time to time, though, she couldn't help but glance Mark's way, and on each occasion she saw that he was always with a different partner. He was certainly doing his best to keep his parents' guests entertained.

'Your glass is empty.' Mark's voice sounded close to her ear, and she felt a ripple of awareness run through her. 'Let me get you another drink.' He alerted a waiter and handed her another glass.

'Thank you.' She glanced at him over the rim of the fluted goblet. 'I think I'll take my time with this one,' she said, looking around for a ledge to rest it on. 'I've had two or three already.'

His mouth curved in a smile. 'Then perhaps we could dance?' he murmured. He took the champagne from her and placed it on a narrow shelf, and then held out his hand to her.

She hesitated and he sent her a probing glance. 'I know you have doubts about me,' he murmured, 'but shall we put aside our differences for now and take to the floor?'

Without realising quite how it had happened, she found herself on the dance floor a moment later, held within his gentle embrace, whirling to the lilting music of a waltz. How was it that the rhythm had changed in that instant from fast to slow and dreamy?

Mark's hand clasped hers firmly, and his other hand rested lightly on the curve of her back, leading her with a sure touch, while his thighs brushed hers in a sensual movement that stirred her senses and made her head spin.

His nearness robbed her of strength. Her limbs were suddenly weak, insubstantial like thistledown, and it seemed to Sarah that she was walking on air. He swirled her around the dance floor effortlessly, and she was so close to him that her nervous system went into overdrive and she found that she could scarcely breathe. When the music finally came to an end, she looked up at him bemusedly, robbed of words, still feeling as though she was floating among clouds.

His gaze meshed with hers. 'More champagne?' he asked.

'I don't think I should,' she murmured. She was already fizzing, heady with the sensation of being held, of being locked in his embrace.

The rest of the evening flashed by in a flurry of lights and music and delicious sensation. Mark was attentive, making sure that she had everything she needed, introducing her to his family and friends. Perhaps he felt obliged to, because he had persuaded her here against her will, or it could be that he empathised with her in some way because of what had happened to Hannah.

He introduced her to his father, a distinguished-looking man, tall and strong, his hair greying at the temples, his manner courteous and attentive. She enquired about the fundraising.

'I must say that I'm pleased with the way things have gone this evening,' he told her.

'We've collected more donations than we could have imagined.'

He was a straightforward man, likeable and without airs, and he didn't seem at all like the ruthless businessman Owen had made him out to be. Even so, she wondered how he had managed to achieve all these trappings of wealth and power. Had he really been responsible for engineering his son's promotion?

She said, 'Have you always had an interest in helping the hospital, or are you especially involved with the renal unit?'

'I try to help out with various charities where I can,' he said. 'Last year we raised money for the world disaster fund, and this year we're concentrating on the local hospital. It seemed especially relevant since Mark was looking to work there.'

'I see.' She was quiet, thinking about that. Was there some truth in what Owen had said?

Mark had been standing with his mother, saying goodbye to guests who were getting ready to leave, but after a minute or two he came over and took Sarah to one side.

'Are you all right?' he asked.

She nodded. 'I think it's time that I was heading home,' she murmured. She wouldn't be out of place, doing that. One or two people were beginning to drift away, making preparations for the journey home. Most of them had to be at work in the morning.

He frowned. 'Do you have to go now?'

'I'm afraid so. I need to get up early to get Jamie to school on time. You don't have to trouble yourself, though. Stay here and help your parents with their guests. I'll call a taxi.'

'No, I won't hear of you doing that. Just give me a moment, and I'll drive you.'

'It's still pouring with rain out there,' his father said. 'Take care with your driving. It's been raining practically non-stop for some days now, and I heard that there are floods.'

'I'll be careful,' Mark said. He turned to Sarah. 'You needn't worry. I haven't had much to drink, so you'll be safe.'

'I never doubted it,' she murmured.

They drove back along the same route that

they had taken some hours ago, but Mark studied the road ahead and said, frowning, 'It looks as though my father was right. The road has flooded in the time that we've been at the house. We'll have to turn around and go a different way.'

Sarah peered out of the car window into the darkness. It was hard to make out the scenery, but the car headlights picked out a gleaming mass of water ahead of them. She nodded.

Mark turned the car around and they headed back the way they had come, turning off to go a more circular route. 'We'll go over the bridge,' he said. 'That's usually a safe bet.'

Sarah had driven that way many times before. Now, though, as they approached the bridge, she looked out at the cars that were parked along the roadside and she said quietly, 'I'm not sure about this. Why are these cars parked up ahead? They look as though they've been abandoned.'

'I think you're right. That probably means that the road's flooded over there, too.' He slowed the car to a halt. 'I'm going to get out and take a look at what's happening. We should be far enough away from any problems if I park the car back here. I want you to stay inside here where it's warm and dry while I go and look up ahead.'

She wondered why he wasn't just going to turn the car around. 'What is it? Have you seen something? Do you think someone's in trouble?'

He was frowning. 'I can see a car and some lights. I'm not sure what's going on—I can't quite make it out.' He reached into the glove compartment and took out a torch. 'Wait here. I'll be just a few minutes.'

He stepped out of the car and disappeared into the darkness, and Sarah tried to keep track of him and see what was happening. After a minute or two she realised that it was useless. It was pitch black out there, and she couldn't imagine what he was looking for. Unless... Was it possible that someone had not seen the danger and had ventured onwards into the floodwaters?

Sarah pushed open the car door and scrambled out. She heard voices in the distance, muffled sounds, and she struggled to make sense of them. The wind was howling and the rain beat down on her, dampening the light jacket that she was wearing within seconds. She pulled the edges of the jacket around herself and hugged it to her to keep out the cold.

There was no sign of Mark. Then she heard a woman's voice, a ragged sound brutally torn away by the wind. 'Help us, someone help us.'

Another sound followed, floating on the wind, a sob, a moan of distress, a high-pitched note. Sarah frowned. Surely that cry could only have come from a child?

She rushed towards that sound. There was only the light of the moon to guide her, and all around was just the sweep of the road and the hedgerow on either side. There were open fields along this stretch, she recalled, but now she saw a silver glitter rippling along the road surface, and she knew that she was looking at the river. Horrified, she stared at the swollen surge of water. The river must have broken its banks because now it flowed across her path, and as she stepped forward it came and lapped at her feet, splashing upwards over her legs. She caught her breath as the shock of ice cold water hit her.

The moon dipped behind a cloud and she was plunged into darkness. There was that sound again—a child's voice, a plea for help. Where was it coming from? Where was Mark?

Sarah plunged forward, heedless of the water swirling around her legs. The current was fast, shocking in its power, and she knew that she had to find that child before it was too late. Some dreadful instinct told her that time was running out.

'Where are you? Call out to me. Let me know where you are.' She moved onwards, her legs dragging as the force of the water tried to push her back. It was rising as she battled on, and now it almost reached her waist, making her shudder, her body shaking with cold.

The cry came again, more faint this time, losing power as though it was being swallowed up, and she turned towards the sound. 'Try to hold on,' she called. 'I'm coming. I'll get you.'

She could hear the rush of water now, and she looked around and despaired. Then the moon came into view once more, and Sarah let her glance move over the expanse of water in front of her and all around her. She caught a brief glimpse of something light-coloured then it disappeared. What was that? Was it a child? She waded towards it.

Bending low, she reached down. Her fingers encountered something cold and clammy, and she suddenly felt sick. It was a child's body tossed casually by the raging water against the hedgerow in a tangle of arms and legs. Sarah stared down at the child and saw a girl's face, lifeless, staring blankly upwards. She bent and gathered her up in her arms, but the small figure was limp like a rag doll and chilled to the bone.

'Sarah?' Mark's voice came to her from several feet away. She looked around but she couldn't see him. Hearing his voice made her realise that he was safe at least, and that knowl-edge helped to sustain her.

'I'm here,' she said, her voice thready. 'I've found a child. I'm going to try and get her back to dry ground.'

'I'll get to you as soon as I can.'

She struggled to hold the child aloft while she battled the surge of water. Her limbs felt like lead, and she had to halt in order to steady herself every now and again, but she focussed on getting back to Mark's car. He had parked it well away from the water, and she needed to get there fast.

At last she reached drier ground. Here she was safe from the floodwater, and she laid the little girl down on the verge, kneeling down beside her, struggling to get her breath after her exertions.

The child seemed to be about six years old, she reckoned, but she wasn't breathing and there was no pulse, and Sarah was panicky with the thought that there was nothing she could do to save her.

She checked the little girl's mouth for debris and then, when she was satisfied that it was clear, she tilted the child's head back a little, and breathed into her mouth, stopping to press down on her chest with the palm of her hand every now and again. She continued like that for some time, fearing that it was already too late, but unwilling to give up.

There was a movement beside her, and she looked up to see that Mark had returned. He was carrying a woman, and now he laid her down carefully alongside the girl.

'Is she still alive?' Mark looked at the child, his expression etched with concern.

'She isn't breathing. I'm doing what I can for her. Have you called for an ambulance?' She went on with the compressions while she was talking, then blew air into the child's mouth once more.

'Yes, I did that as soon as I saw that the mother was in a bad way.' Mark was walking around to the back of his car and Sarah heard him open the boot. He came back a moment later and placed an oxygen mask over the woman's face.

'How is she doing?' Sarah asked.

'She's breathing, and she seems to be coming round now. She must have stumbled and lost her footing somehow, because when I found her she was lying slumped across a low-lying tree branch. There's a gash on her head, and I think she must have been knocked out for a while.'

The woman moved, trying to push the mask away. 'Where's Vicky?' she managed. 'My little girl—what's happening to her?'

'We have her here and we're doing what we can for her,' Mark said. 'Try not to upset yourself and concentrate on breathing deeply.'

The child suddenly spluttered but then lay still, and Sarah caught her breath. 'I need to intubate her,' she said. 'Do you have an airway in your car?'

'Yes, I brought my emergency kit from the boot. It's here.' He shone the torch so that Sarah could see what she was doing, and now she worked quickly and carefully to insert the endotracheal tube and airway. As soon as she'd finished, she covered the girl's mouth with the mask and ventilation bag and started to apply positive pressure, pumping oxygen into the child's lungs.

'I'll get some blankets,' Mark said. 'The ambulance should be here any minute.'

They did what they could to keep the mother and child warm until the ambulance came. The little girl was in a bad way but at least she was breathing now. Sarah was afraid that she was suffering from hypothermia and they needed to get her to hospital quickly. Her spirits lifted when she heard the ambulance in the distance.

The paramedics worked quickly to attend to their patients, and Sarah went with them in the ambulance so that she could look after the little girl on the journey. The mother appeared to be stable for the moment.

'I'll follow you in the car,' Mark said.

Once they were at the hospital, the emergency team took over. 'We need to get both of them warmed up,' the doctor said. 'Perhaps you should go and get yourselves dried out. We'll let you know what's happening.'

Sarah looked down at her once beautiful blue dress. It was streaked with dirt and soaked through, and she was shivering with cold. Mark hadn't fared any better. He, too, was wet through and through, and he sent her a rueful glance.

'He's probably right.'

'I'm not going anywhere until I know that the little girl is all right,' she said.

He nodded, but turned away and left the room for a moment. A short time later he was back, and he draped a blanket around Sarah's shoulders. 'You're wetter than the fish in my pond,' he murmured. 'I thought I told you to stay in the car while I checked things out.'

'I'm glad that I didn't.'

He gave a crooked grin. 'Actually, so am I. I saw that the woman's car had been abandoned in the middle of the flow of water. The doors were open, and I realised that she had been in her car when she was caught up in the flood.

She must have decided to walk to safety with her daughter, but the sudden rush of water overwhelmed them as the river burst its banks. I found the woman and managed to lift her clear, but I didn't know about the little girl until it was too late. She must have been swept along with the current.'

'Do you think that they'll be all right?'

'I do. The child probably survived because the water was so cold. It slows the metabolism and helps to prevent damage to the brain. They're both in good hands now. I'm sure that they'll come through this.'

The emergency doctor agreed with him. He came and found them some time later and said, 'We're going to admit both of them for observation, but things are looking good. We've been attempting to bring their temperatures back to normal, and they've started to respond to treatment. I don't think that they'll have suffered any ill effects from this.' He smiled. 'It was lucky for them that you two happened to be around at the time. If I were you, I would go home and get yourselves warmed up.'

Mark nodded. 'Thanks for letting us know.' He glanced at Sarah. 'He's right in what he says. It's time that I was getting you home. If you stay in those cold wet things for much longer, you'll end up in a hospital bed yourself.'

He turned her around and led her away. She was still wrapped up in the blanket, but when they went out into the corridor he put his arms around her and hugged her close. She guessed that he was just trying to instil some heat into her, but all the same it felt good to have him hold her that way. He was strong and protective and she wanted to stay locked in his arms for a long, long time.

CHAPTER FIVE

'WHERE are we going?' Sarah peered out of the car window into the darkness, trying to work out the route that they were taking, but Mark had turned the car off the main road. She didn't know this road. 'This isn't the way to my father's house.' She shivered, her clothes clinging to her damply and sending a chill through her despite the covering blanket.

Mark shot her a quick glance. 'It'll be quicker if we go to my house first. It's only five minutes away, and I think it will be better if we get you warm and dry as soon as possible. I'll make sure that you get back home, don't worry.'

'I didn't realise that you lived this close to the hospital. I always thought that you had a house out in the country.'

'I did, but when I took over as consultant I decided that I would be better off with something nearer. I was lucky in that this house came on the market at the right time. It's still fairly rural and when I saw it I realised that it was just what I was looking for.'

He turned the car onto a country lane and a little while later he slowed down and said, 'Here we are.'

He pulled into a wide driveway, and when Sarah stepped out of the car and looked around she saw that lanterns illuminated the porch and the side of the house, providing a welcoming glow.

It was a sprawling building, stone built, with roofs set at different levels and lovely Georgian windows overlooking the fields opposite. The house was colour-washed with white paint and bordered by an array of shrubs and climbing plants. A low wall, also painted white, fronted the building and enclosed a neat cottage garden.

Sarah didn't see many other houses around,

and this one nestled comfortably in a corner of the rural landscape, set back from the road.

She stared for a moment. 'It's beautiful,' she said. A gust of cold wind ran through her and she shivered, pulling the blanket more closely around her.

'Come on, let's get you inside.' He led the way, opening the front door and showing her into a wide hall. 'Through here,' he murmured, indicating a room off the hall.

It was a large sitting room, warm from central heating, but he went and lit the fire at the hearth so that the glow of flame brightened up the room. She went and stood in front of the fireplace, letting the warmth surround her.

Mark said, 'I'll go and make us a hot drink, and I'll see if I can find a change of clothes for you. I can let you have a T-shirt and an over-shirt and a sweater, probably, and there should be some of my cousin's jeans around some-where. She's about your size.'

'Does your cousin stay here sometimes, then?'

He nodded. 'She came for a visit recently with my uncle and aunt. We all get on well together and they decided to stay for a few days because they wanted to do a bit of shopping over the weekend. There are enough rooms here for me to accommodate them easily enough. After they had gone home I noticed that Carol had left a few odds and ends behind. I phoned her about them, but she said not to worry. I know that she won't mind if you borrow them.'

He glanced at her searchingly. 'You know, you're welcome to stay, if you'd like. It's very late, and you must be worn out by now.'

She shook her head. 'I don't think I'd better do that.'

He frowned. 'Are you sure? You don't have to be at work in the morning, do you?'

'No, but Jamie will wake up and wonder where I am. I don't want to change his routine any more than necessary. He's been through more than enough changes lately.'

'That's true, I suppose.' He waved her to an

armchair. 'Why don't you sit down for a while and try to get warm, while I go and organise things?'

She did as he had suggested, enjoying the heat from the fire, and he was back within a couple of minutes, bearing a steaming cup of hot chocolate. 'Drink that,' he said, 'then I can show you the bathroom, and you can get changed if you'd like.'

'Thanks.' She nodded, sipping gratefully at the drink. 'You're soaked through yourself,' she said. 'The same applies to you—you ought to get into something dry.'

He nodded. 'I will in a while. Let's just get you sorted out first.'

He showed her to the bathroom a few minutes later. 'Take your time,' he said. 'You can shower or take a bath, if you'd like. There are fresh towels in the cupboard.'

'Thanks, I think I'll do that.' She looked down at herself. 'I'll be glad to wash away some of the grime.'

He nodded and gave a quick smile. 'Help

yourself to whatever you need, and come downstairs when you're ready. There's no need to rush. I'm going to take a shower in the other bathroom along the hall.'

Sarah took her time bathing. It was good to lie back in the warm water and feel the heat seep back into her body. She looked around the room as she lay there. It was a sumptuous bathroom, the height of luxury, beautifully tiled, with glass shelving and fittings that gleamed. Everything about Mark's home was perfect.

When she had finished bathing, she dried herself and began to dress. There was a fresh pack of underwear, still in the Cellophane wrapper, and she guessed his cousin must have left this behind, too, after her shopping spree. She would buy replacements for her.

Mark was in the kitchen when she went back downstairs. It was a large, square room, with every modern appliance you could wish for and an array of fitted cupboards and work surfaces. It was all smooth lines and tiled surfaces, with lovely touches in the decorative corner units and ornately carved shelving nooks.

He looked at her and smiled. 'Do you feel better for that?' He checked her over. 'The jeans aren't a bad fit, are they? My shirt might be a bit oversized, but it looks great on you.'

She made a wry face. 'I feel much more human now, thanks.' He didn't look bad himself. He had changed into chinos and a casual shirt, and he looked fresh and clean and full of energy once more. How did he manage it when these were the early hours of the morning? She was a wreck. She might look all right on the outside, but her nerves had been shattered after what she had gone through.

She put her wet clothes down on a corner of the work surface. 'Do you have a plastic bag that I could put these in? I think I'll be throwing them away, but a bag will keep them from making more of a mess till I get them home.'

'Of course.' He reached for a bag from a cupboard and said, 'I've made you some hot soup. Come and sit down and drink it. It will help to keep the warmth in.' He waved a hand to the table and pushed a mug forward.

'Thanks.'

He placed the clothes in a bag while she seated herself at the island bar in the middle of the kitchen and sipped at the hot liquid. 'It was a shame about your lovely dress,' he commented, 'but I can't help thinking that it was worth it.' He smiled, looking into her eyes. 'I'm glad that we went to the bridge. I don't like to think what would have happened if we'd gone another way.'

She nodded. 'So am I.' She was sad about her beautiful dress, but there was no doubt that it was beyond redemption.

He came over to her. 'You were very brave out there. You must have been terrified but you didn't give up and you went on trying to find the little girl. You saved her. Doesn't that make you feel good about yourself?'

She made a face. 'I'm glad that she's safe, but I'm not sure that I feel any different about myself. I wasn't able to help my sister, or save Ryan. He's showing no signs of recovery. He's helpless. If anything, though, it's made me realise that I need to be back at work. At least when I'm busy there are moments when I'm not thinking about what happened to them.'

'The child is alive because of you. You should think about that.'

She put her mug down on the table and he came and stood behind her and laid his hands on her shoulders. It was a warm, comforting feeling to have him close by, and she savoured the moment, appreciating the gentle touch of his hands.

She said quietly, 'Maybe. I'm glad that I was there for her at the right time, but really my efforts weren't any greater than yours. After all, you saved her mother, didn't you?'

He studied her for a moment. 'Why is it so difficult for you to feel positive about what you do? You're the same at work. You have absolutely no confidence in yourself, have you?'

She frowned. How did he know that? All this time she had believed she had managed to hide her doubts from him and put on a reasonably good front, and yet he must have known she had misgivings all along.

She said slowly, 'I've never been sure that I was cut out for emergency medicine. I do my best, but I'm always afraid that I'll make a mistake. In our job, we can't afford to make errors of judgement, can we?'

'What makes you think that you're any different from anyone else? We all make mistakes at some time or other. It's human nature to be fallible.'

His hands caressed her shoulders, gently massaging them as though he would ease the tension from her, and she wondered if he knew what effect he was having on her. Probably not, she decided. It was just an absent-minded gesture on his part, a subconscious desire to make her feel better, nothing more, but it filled her with awareness of him, and made her wish that she could lean her head back against his chest and absorb his strength and support.

'I've never known you to make a mistake,'

she said, 'but I've made so many…the man with the tumour, the other day. My sister's boyfriend, Ryan. I didn't do anything about his head injury and that's why he's in a coma now. Perhaps I should have taken more note of his deteriorating level of consciousness and given him medication to lower the intracranial pressure. If I had acted sooner, he might not be in the condition he is now.'

'You did what you could for him at the time. You needed to concentrate all your efforts on his other, more immediate injuries, and you shouldn't blame yourself for his condition now. He's lucky to be alive.'

She doubted whether Mark would have been remiss as she had been. He always managed to think on several fronts at once. 'I don't think my sister will see things that way. When she comes to question why he's not responding to treatment, she'll want to know how it came about.'

'I think you're being too hard on yourself.' He gently turned her around so that she swivelled in her chair to face him. 'Why do you punish yourself this way?'

'Don't you agree with my judgement of myself?' she countered. 'When we were at the monthly meeting the other day, talking about ways to increase throughput in A and E, you had no qualms about dismissing my objections to Shaun's suggestion. I had the feeling that you didn't rate my comments very highly. You seemed to be very much taken with Shaun's ideas and ready to casually disregard mine.'

'You feel that way because you don't know me very well.' His mouth made a wry shape. 'I believe in challenging people, in making them think, trying to draw the best out of them.'

'I think maybe you went about it the wrong way with me. I'm not good at cynicism and confrontation. I'm more for working as a team and helping each other out where necessary.'

'There's nothing wrong with that.' His mouth curved into a crooked smile. 'It's pretty much the way I think, too.' He looked into her eyes for a moment, and then, leaning forward, he dropped a light kiss on her mouth. She was so stunned by his unexpected action that her eyes widened and her lips parted in dazed wonderment.

He was very still, looking at her consideringly, and he must have decided that the experience was worth repeating because he moved closer and drew her to him, kissing her with a thoroughness that took her breath away. She closed her eyes and absorbed the sensation, feeling the tingling response of her lips and an answering heat that rippled through the length of her body. His hands moved over her, shaping her to him.

It felt unbelievably good and she melted into his embrace, wanting the kiss to go on and on. It was madness, of course, but she had never known this deep-seated feeling of belonging in her life before, and it all seemed so right, so perfectly natural.

She was lost, taken up with absorbing this irresistible wave of new sensation, so that when he finally dragged his mouth from hers she felt the loss as keenly as if he had taken her into the middle of an ice rink and left her there.

She opened her eyes and stared up at him, startled, enchanted, tantalised and wanting more, but she was so bemused by what had happened that she said nothing, Instead, she simply watched him and wondered what could have drawn him to do that.

He stepped away from her. 'I don't know,' he said, as though she had spoken. 'Don't ask. I've no idea what came over me.' He looked as though he was almost as mystified as she was.

He backed away some more, looking at her guardedly. She still hadn't recovered enough to say anything and he added, 'Perhaps it happened because we shared so much tonight, stumbling across the mother and child that way. All sorts of thoughts go through your head at a time like that. You begin to take account of what's important and what isn't. It makes you realise that life can be snatched away in a second or two.'

At last she came to her senses. She straightened. 'I think I know what you mean,' she said haltingly. 'There are moments that make you stand still and take stock. I think that's what happened with me one time—why I realised that I wanted to be a doctor, and why I wanted to do well in emergency medicine.'

His brows drew together in a dark line. 'What happened? Did some special event make you decide what you wanted to do?'

She swallowed and then nodded. 'My mother was killed in a car accident some years back, and it broke my heart that no one had been there to save her. It all happened so suddenly, and it was heart-rending, the way she was taken from us without any warning. Something like that tends to make you adjust your priorities.'

He nodded. 'That's understandable.'

'Yes…well…' She stood up, uncertain all at once. 'I really should get back to Jamie. I know my dad's there with him, but Jamie tends to look for me in the mornings, and life's been up-setting enough for him lately. I don't want to disrupt him any more than is necessary.'

'Of course. I'll take you home.'

He was as good as his word, and Sarah

slipped into her father's house just a short time later. Her father and Jamie were fast asleep, and she crept into her own room without disturbing them.

In the morning, Sarah was glad she wasn't on duty that day. Too many thoughts were going round in her head, slowing up her reactions. As it was, she managed to get Jamie to school on time, and then she did a few chores around the house before going with her father to see her sister and Ryan at the hospital.

She didn't see Mark, but she guessed he was busy at work in A and E.

They collected Jamie from school on their way back home, and Sarah started to make preparations for tea. She was laying the table in the kitchen when a visitor walked into the room and startled her.

'Sarah? Your father let me in. He said you were in the middle of doing something and that it was all right for me to come through.'

Sarah looked up, and her jaw dropped when she saw Owen standing in front of her. He was a head taller than she was, with dark hair, strands of it falling across his brow.

Recovering after a moment or two, she said, 'Owen, I had no idea you were coming over here. How are you? Is this just a fleeting visit, or do you have some time off?'

'I'm on my way to a meeting at the conference centre, and I thought I would drop by and see how you were doing. Has there been any news of Hannah and Ryan?'

She shook her head. 'We've heard nothing specific yet. They're going to do some tests on Hannah tomorrow to see if she's recovered any sensation yet, but Ryan is still deep in a coma. It's all been very upsetting.'

'I can imagine.' He came over to her and put his arms around her, and Sarah was surprised by how little response she felt towards him. Perhaps he would have kissed her, but she turned her face to one side to avoid the possibility. She didn't want him to get the wrong idea.

Had she really once thought that she might have a future with him? Perhaps it had only been that they were friends, with a similar outlook on life and an easygoing attitude towards each other. Over these last few months she had come to realise that there had been nothing more to their relationship than a comfortable companionship, and that was no way near enough.

A sound from the kitchen door alerted her and made her half turn in that direction. She saw Jamie come bounding into the room from the garden, with Kingston close on his heels.

'Nantie Sarah, can Kingston come with me to the hospital to see Mummy?'

Sarah shook her head. 'I'm sorry, Jamie, but they don't let dogs into hospitals. You could tell Mummy about all the things that Kingston gets up to, though. She would like that.'

Jamie's mouth turned down at the corners. Then he saw that Sarah was not alone, and he looked up at Owen and studied him for a moment. Next to him, the dog stood very still, a warning growl sounding in his throat as he, too, watched Owen.

'Stop it, Kingston,' Sarah admonished him. The dog stood his ground, continuing to growl, but on a lower note this time.

Sarah eased herself away from Owen. 'It must be that he's not used to you,' she said apologetically. 'He won't hurt you, I'm sure.'

Owen didn't look convinced, and Sarah went over to the dog. 'Owen's a friend,' she told him, stroking his head. 'Be nice.'

Kingston put his head on one side, as though he was trying to weigh things up. He gave a final growl, more in grumpiness than anything else, as if to say, Just be warned. There's more where that came from.

Owen moved away from the table and backed up against the kitchen cupboard. 'Perhaps I'll go and talk to your father for a while,' he said.

Sarah nodded. 'All right. I'll come and join you in a minute or two.'

She looked at Jamie. He was trying to filch a cake from the table, and she told him, 'Go and wash your hands first, young man.'

He went off good-naturedly, and the dog

settled down by the kitchen door. Sarah frowned. It was strange that he should react that way with Owen. When he had first met Mark he had been more than happy to greet him.

Owen stayed and had tea with them, and when they were finishing off the remains of the fruit pie that she had made he said, 'You know, Sarah, I've been watching you with little Jamie, and it seems to me that you're really good with him. I think you're good with the children at the hospital, too. Haven't you ever thought about going in for paediatrics?'

Jamie had finished his meal, and Sarah had sent him to play with his cars in the dining room. She could see him from the kitchen through the open doorway. 'I've thought about it,' she said. 'I'm not sure—it can be rewarding, working with children, but it can be heartbreaking, too.'

'There's always a down side to being a doctor,' Owen said, 'but I think this would be an ideal career move for you.' He turned to her father. 'Don't you agree?'

'I'm sure that Sarah would be good at whatever she chooses to do,' her father said. 'She puts her best into everything. I think it's probably too early for her to decide just yet. She still has to finish her stint in A and E.'

Owen shook his head. 'It might seem as though there's plenty of time for her to make up her mind, but these things often have to be sorted out in advance, and I think it's always wise to seize opportunities when they arrive.' He hesitated, glancing at Sarah. 'There's a vacancy coming up at my hospital fairly soon,' he said. 'They're looking for a recently quali-fied doctor to take up a paediatric posting, and I'm fairly sure that you would make the grade, if you wanted to apply for it. You did really well in your paediatric placement at this hospital, didn't you?'

Sarah frowned. 'I suppose I did, but I'm not sure what I want to do at the moment. With Hannah and Ryan being in such a bad way, I'm finding it hard to think about anything too deeply.'

'I understand that, but you don't have to decide right away,' Owen countered. 'I could put a word in for you, though. If you want to work with children, I'm sure something can be arranged, and it would be great to have you working alongside me again. I'd like you to come with me.'

'I don't think I'm going to be leaving here,' Sarah said. 'I need to be close to my family.'

'I know that. I do understand, but this job isn't going to be available for a month or so yet. By then Hannah and Ryan could both have made a recovery.'

'Maybe. I'll think about it,' Sarah said. She looked around and saw that Jamie was standing in the doorway, watching them. He came into the room and put a toy car down on the table in front of his grandad.

'The wheels have come off,' he said. 'Can you mend it for me?'

Her father picked up the toy. 'Let's have a look,' he murmured.

Sarah stood up and began to clear the plates

from the table. She stacked them in the dish-washer and Owen came to help. She glanced at him. Was he hoping that the two of them would get back together again? Was that what was behind this visit? Somehow or other she would have to explain to him that it wasn't going to happen.

She broached the subject just before he was about to leave. They were alone in the living room, and she tried to make him understand that she would always be his friend, but nothing more than that.

His expression was rueful. 'I think I realised that when I left to take up my new job. You tried to tell me then, but I sort of lived in hope for a while.'

'I'm sorry if I've hurt you,' she said softly, 'but I didn't want you to get the wrong idea.'

'I know. I understand—but it makes no difference about the job. I still think it would be a good idea, and I think you would make a terrific children's doctor. I don't want you to dismiss the idea out of hand.'

'I won't. You'll have to give me time, though. I have too many things on my mind just now.'

He frowned. 'I hope that things go well for Hannah—Ryan, too. Sometimes people come out of comas quite unexpectedly, you know. It could help, of course, if you keep talking to him and try to stimulate him with familiar voices and sounds.'

Sarah had already been doing that. She had visited Ryan on several occasions, and had even taken Jamie with her once or twice. It had been difficult to know whether Jamie would be upset, seeing his father so helpless, but he had reacted reasonably well.

She took Jamie with her to the hospital the next day. While her father was visiting Hannah, she took him to Ryan's room, and she chatted quietly to Ryan as though he could hear what she was saying. There was no response.

Jamie said, 'Is my daddy going to get better?'

'I hope so,' Sarah said. 'The doctors and nurses are all looking after him. He loves you, you know.'

The little boy nodded, but he was quiet for a while and then he said, 'Can we go and see my mummy now?'

'Of course.' She held out her hand to him and then said goodbye to Ryan.

She and Jamie walked to Hannah's room and joined her father. A few minutes later Mark put his head around the door and Sarah felt her heart give a funny little jump.

'Do you mind if I come and say hello?' he asked.

Sarah shook her head, and he approached Hannah, smiling. 'How are you feeling?' he asked. 'Is everyone treating you well?'

Hannah was lying flat on the bed. 'I'm all right,' she said. 'I think they're going to do some tests today. I'm not sure, but I think I can feel some tingling in my spine. They said that's a good sign.'

Mark nodded. 'It is. You should be pleased about that.'

'Maybe, but I'm not sure about anything. I still can't feel my legs, and I can't go home and be with Jamie, and then there's Ryan—he's very ill and I don't understand how it could have happened. One minute we were driving along and talking, and the next we were both being brought to hospital. I just can't take it all in.'

'You need to give yourself more time,' her father put in. 'You've been through an awful lot and it's bound to make you feel low. It's difficult for anyone to comprehend.'

They talked for a while, and when it was time for Jamie to leave so that his mother could rest, Sarah led the child away, and Mark went with them. As before, her father stayed for a while with Hannah.

'I'm on my way back to A and E,' Mark said, 'but I'll walk with you as far as the café.' They turned into the corridor, and he added, 'It's good for Hannah to see Jamie, even if it's for just a short time. It will help her with the physiotherapy, and give her more of a reason to work on her recovery.'

'I know. She loves to see him.'

Jamie looked up at Mark. 'I like it when I

come to see Mummy. Can I bring Kingston with me next time? Nantie Sarah says no, but you could let me, couldn't you?'

'I'm sorry, Jamie,' Mark said, 'but dogs aren't allowed in hospital. What you could do, though, is help get Kingston ready for when your mummy comes home. Perhaps you could teach him how to fetch things for her, or make him sit when you tell him. Your mummy will be pleased if he's really good, won't she?'

Jamie nodded. 'You like Kingston, don't you?'

'I do.' Mark smiled at him. 'So does Auntie Sarah.'

'I know.' Jamie frowned, and then the frown was replaced with an impish grin. 'Owen doesn't like Kingston.'

'Doesn't he?' It was Mark's turn to frown. 'Why do you think that?'

'He had to go out of the kitchen 'cos Kingston growled at him. Kingston doesn't like Owen. Owen wants to take Nantie Sarah away, and Kingston doesn't want her to go.'

Sarah was startled. Had Jamie heard their conversation in the kitchen yesterday and put two and two together?

Mark's dark brow rose. 'Oh, I see.' He obviously didn't, because a crooked line etched its way into his forehead. He glanced at Sarah. 'I take it that Owen has been to see you?'

'Yes. He was on his way to a meeting and he stopped by the house.'

'So what's this about him taking you away?'

Sarah lifted her shoulders in an awkward gesture. 'He mentioned a job opportunity that was coming up—a post in paediatrics at his hospital. He thought perhaps I should apply for it.'

'Doesn't he know that you still have to finish your contract here? Is he trying to poach my staff?'

Sarah's mouth made an odd shape. For a brief moment she had dared to hope that he might not want to lose her for reasons other than work, but of course she was fooling herself. 'He just thought that I might be interested.

When this posting comes to an end, I'll have to look for something else.'

'You could go on working in A and E, couldn't you?'

'I suppose so, but I'm not sure what I want to do. I'm not convinced that I'd make a good A and E doctor. Perhaps I need to look around for alternatives.' She was wistful for a second or two. 'I did enjoy my stint in Paediatrics.'

Mark was still frowning, and she guessed that he didn't like the idea of Owen trying to persuade people to move away from the hospital. She doubted that there was much he could do about it.

They had arrived at the café, and his bleeper suddenly sounded. He drew it from his pocket, glanced down at it and said, 'I should go. Things are turning out to be more hectic than usual today.' He looked as though he was reluctant to leave them, but he knelt down and had a quick word with Jamie and then straightened. Looking at Sarah, he said, 'I expect I'll see you tomorrow, won't I? You said that you felt ready to come back to work.'

'Yes, I did. I'll be there.'

She was glad to be getting back to work. It was good to be able to keep busy.

She had been on duty for some time the next day when a spate of patients suffering from violence-related injuries started to come in.

Mark came out of a treatment room and walked towards her. 'There was a football game at the local stadium this afternoon,' he said, 'and it looks as though we're getting the fallout from that. The police have come along with one or two of our customers.'

He handed her a chart. 'You can take the patient in treatment room two. You probably need to check for fractures.' He glanced at her, adding, 'You should take care. Some of these people are a bit fractious.'

'I will.' Sarah went into the treatment room and carefully examined her patient. His nose was a mess. Apart from the general disfigurement, there was bleeding and tenderness and she was concerned about the swelling, which was obstructing the nasal passage.

'Were you in a fight?' she asked.

'You shub shee the ubber one,' he managed.

Sarah didn't quite make out the words, but she guessed the other man in the scuffle hadn't come out of it too well.

'Andy,' she murmured, 'it looks as though you have a broken nose, and I'm a little concerned about some of the swelling. I think it might be what we call a septal haematoma—which is a collection of blood that can cause certain problems.'

Andy stared at her. 'Ig thab dab?' he asked. He was holding tissues to his bloody nose.

'Is that bad?' she repeated, and he nodded. 'Well,' she murmured, 'it could be, if it isn't treated straight away. I'll need to give you antibiotics to prevent any infection setting in and I'll make sure that you have something for the pain. The X-ray film isn't particularly helpful, so I'm going to send you for a CT scan.'

'Dow?'

'Yes, right away. That will give us a better picture of what's happened, and then, if my diagnosis is correct, you'll need to see an ENT surgeon who will drain the blood that's causing the swelling, and then he'll be able to realign the broken bone.'

She turned to the nurse in attendance and said, 'We'll give him ibuprofen for the pain. He needs to go for the scan now, and I'll see him when he gets back.'

'OK.' The nurse turned away and Andy started to get to his feet.

'No,' Sarah said. 'You should sit down. We'll put you in a wheelchair, to be on the safe side, in case you've sustained any kind of head injury.'

He subsided into the chair, and the nurse wheeled him out of the room. Sarah followed, and as she moved to the desk to write out the relevant forms, a huge man came out of nowhere and almost knocked her over. He had a cut and bruised eye, and there was a considerable amount of swelling, so that he was squinting as he looked at Andy. He looked as though he was spoiling for a fight.

'What's he doing here?' he growled, his expression furious. 'Let me get at him.' He started towards her patient, and Sarah hurriedly intervened.

'You shouldn't be here,' she said. 'This is a restricted area.'

'Not to me, it isn't. I'm not letting him get away with it.' He pushed Sarah forcefully out of the way, sending her flying into the desk, and then made to lunge at Andy, who was out of the chair by now and ready to fight all over again.

Sarah was winded, but she shouted for Security and then went back to remonstrate with the man. He made a grab for her arm and missed, but then swung her around and sent her thudding against a trolley. The trolley swivelled and crashed into a wall. She crumpled, the breath knocked out of her as she hit the metal bar, and she banged her head as she fell.

'What's going on here?' Mark had appeared and he took hold of her assailant by the collar.

Taken unawares, the man was spun around and forced against the wall, his cheek pressed up against the noticeboard and his flailing arm twisted behind him.

'We don't tolerate that kind of behaviour in here,' Mark ground out. 'You should take your temper outside and cool off.'

Security arrived, and the man was bundled away, cursing and resisting with every step. Sarah had managed to scramble to her feet, and now she supported herself against the trolley and looked at Mark, astonished by the swift moves he had made and the sureness of his touch.

'Where did you learn to do that?' she gasped, struggling for breath.

'Martial arts classes,' he answered. 'Are you all right?'

She nodded. 'I'm fine.' She tried to straighten up, but a wave of dizziness swamped her and she realised that her head was sore and a vein in her temple was thumping.

'You don't look it,' he said, his mouth set in a grim line. He came over to her and put a supportive hand under her elbow as she went to move towards her patient.

'Shaun will take over here. You're on a break as of now.'

She made to object but he led her away, taking her back into the treatment room that she had just left and sitting her down in a chair. He shut the door behind them.

'Did you bang your ribs?' he asked. 'Let me see.'

'No way,' she said, holding on to her shirt when he would have lifted it. 'I was just winded for a while, that's all.'

His mouth made a crooked line. 'All right,' he conceded, 'but you've a nasty gash on your temple. I'll deal with that for you.'

She sat quietly while he cleaned up the wound. He was gentle, his touch light, and he did everything in a relaxed, unhurried way, as though he wanted to give her time to get herself together.

'It's not too bad,' he said, taping a dressing in place. 'You might have a headache for a while, but there's no major damage.'

'I must look a mess,' she said awkwardly.

He gave her a rueful smile. 'Isn't that just typical of a woman? She starts to worry about her looks.' He shook his head. 'I think you'll be fine...your hair will cover most of it. It always was a riotous affair, and your curls are falling down over it already. You'll look as beautiful as ever before too long.'

She sent him a swift, shaken glance. Did he really think that she was beautiful? His mouth slanted, and she came to her senses with a feeling of letdown. No, of course he didn't. He was just trying to make her feel better about things.

'Thank you for coming and helping me,' she said huskily. 'I was so afraid. He looked fearsome and I didn't know what to do. You were wonderful. I was terrified.'

He put out a hand and stroked her cheek, his thumb gently brushing her soft skin. 'I'm not surprised. You shouldn't have to deal with those sorts of situations. You're a doctor, not a bouncer.'

'But we have to, don't we? I mean, it's part of

the job these days. More and more we find our-selves up against aggressive patients.' Her mouth trembled. 'I'm just not cut out for this. I should have been able to look after my patient, and instead he very nearly suffered another injury.' She began to shake, her whole body suddenly racked with small tremors. She tried to keep herself still, stop herself from falling apart.

Mark hunkered down in front of her and put his arms around her. 'It isn't part of your job to break up fights. It isn't what you're trained for. That's why we have security people.'

'I know. I'm sorry,' she whispered. 'I don't know what's the matter with me.' She knew that she should be stronger, but she was fast losing the battle. A wash of tears came into her eyes.

'You're in shock,' he murmured. 'You need to forget what happened.' He gave a faint smile. 'Let me help you with that.' He leaned forward and kissed her then, a sweet, probing kiss, ex-ploring the softness of her mouth, as though he would coax her to forget all her fears.

Her lips parted and clung to his, drinking in the comfort he offered until she lost sight of her uncertainties and could only think of this wonderful moment in time. His kiss was gentle, claiming her mouth with infinite tenderness, filling her senses with a longing for something that could never be hers.

But he was way out of her league, and his family, his lifestyle were aeons apart from hers. This should not be happening. He was only trying to comfort her. She shouldn't read anything into it.

Reluctantly, he broke off the kiss and leaned back, looking at her with an odd expression. 'Better now?' he asked.

She nodded, and he got slowly to his feet once more. He moved away from her, glancing at her from time to time with a wry twist to his mouth as he tidied away the cotton wool and tape that he had used to clean her wound.

It had been an exercise in taking her mind off things, hadn't it? He had said as much, and she wished that things could be different. She suddenly realised that she wanted him to care, but that wasn't what this was all about. He wasn't affected by the kiss as she was, she was sure of it. It had meant nothing at all, had it?

CHAPTER SIX

'THIS patient needs dialysis,' Mark said, handing a chart back to Sarah. 'Have you been in touch with the renal unit?'

'Yes, I contacted them a while ago. They're going to arrange for him to be admitted. I think things are difficult over in the unit at the moment, but they say that they'll be able to find a place for him. I imagine things will stay troublesome until the new unit opens.' She paused, glancing at the patient. 'Hopefully, he'll only need the dialysis for a short time, until his kidneys recover.'

'It would help if we could get the new dialysis machine installed,' Mark murmured, 'but we need some ideas for additional fundraising.' He made a wry face. 'Shaun suggested that we all do a sponsored run, but I haven't been able to find that many people who are keen to take part.'

Sarah wrote out a prescription for medication and handed it to the nurse who was checking drips and trying to make the patient more comfortable. She told Mark, 'You'd do better to hold some kind of garden fête. Now that the weather is improving, people are more inclined to go out and about, and you might find that they want to go somewhere where they can buy plants for the summer bedding, or look at things on craft stalls. Throw in a dog show and entertainment of some sort, and you might bring in quite a bit of cash.'

He looked at her, his head tilted slightly to one side. 'You know, that's a really good idea.' He smiled, and out of the blue he reached for her and gave her a quick hug, almost lifting her from the floor, so that she gazed up at him with startled eyes. 'I'll have a word with my father,' he said. 'He has enough land to set up something of the kind, and he has contacts, so it shouldn't be too difficult to get the whole thing organised. I'll let you know how we get on.'

She tried an answering smile. He was still holding her, and even the patient was looking at them askance from his bed. She couldn't imagine what the nurse was thinking.

'Do that,' she murmured, feeling embarrassed and exhilarated at the same time. His touch was having a very strange effect on her. It made the blood pound through her veins and she felt a wave of heat surge through her body like a stream of quicksilver. She muttered softly, 'You should put me down. People are looking.'

He laughed. 'That will never do, will it?' All the same, he put her down and then turned to the patient and said with a smile, 'I think our Dr Mitchell has earned her pay for the day. Now, as to your condition, I know that you must be feeling really uncomfortable and quite ill at the moment, and that's because of all the toxins that have built up in your system. You've suffered a very bad infection, but we've managed to isolate the source of the infection and the medication seems to be working now. Once we get you on continuous dialysis, you'll start to feel a lot better, and your kidneys will get a chance to rest and recover.'

The patient managed a smile. 'I hope so.'

Sarah and Mark left the treatment room a moment or two later, and Sarah went to find her next patient. The imprint of Mark's hands stayed with her, even though he had moved away. He appeared to be totally unconcerned, and she tried not to think about him. After all, it had been an instinctive reaction on his part, and he had probably forgotten about it already.

She put all thoughts of the garden fête from her mind, and it seemed like just a few days later when he said, 'How are you fixed for this weekend? My father's managed to set things up for the spring fair, with licences and stallhold-ers and so on, and he's even sorted out the ad-vertising, so we should get a good turnout. He's hoping that you'll enter Kingston for the dog show, and that you'll bring Jamie along to enjoy the roundabout rides. How about it?'

She stared at him. 'You're serious?' she said. She had made the suggestion off the top of her head, but she hadn't really expected anything to come of it, or to find that she was to be involved in any way. The truth was, she hadn't actually thought beyond the idea, and here he was, telling her that he wanted her to be part of it.

'Of course I'm serious. I've already roped in half of the A and E team, the half that isn't on duty, and I had a quick word with your father, and he seemed very keen, though it might have been the mention of the beer tent that encouraged him. I don't see how you can refuse.'

She was open-mouthed. 'When did you talk to my father?'

'This morning, when he came in to visit Hannah. He seemed quite taken with the idea. He said that he would help you out with Kingston.'

'You seem to have thought of everything.'

'Yes, I think so. I certainly hope so.' He lifted a dark brow. 'Is that all settled, then? I could come and pick you up, unless you decide to come along with your father.'

'My dad will bring me,' she said. 'I imagine you'll be far too busy organising things.'

'You could be right.'

Fortunately, on the day of the garden fête the weather turned out to be dry and bright. Mark had been perfectly right when he said there would be a good turnout, but even so, Sarah was amazed by the number of people who milled about the grounds of his father's property.

The last time she had seen his father's house it had been at night, and she hadn't been able to see very much of the grounds. Now, though, she discovered that his land was far more extensive than she ever could have imagined. He had given a great part of it over to the fair, and stalls stretched the length of a field. There was even a bandstand where a group of young men were setting up a drum kit and loudspeakers and were tuning their guitars.

'Wow!' Jamie exclaimed. 'They've got water shooters. Can I have a go, Grandad? Please, Grandad?'

'Of course you can, lad.' Her father turned to Sarah. 'Will you be all right with Kingston while I go and take this young man around?'

She nodded. 'I'll be fine. I think we're expected to take part in the dog show in a few minutes anyway. That should keep us both occupied for a while.'

Mark came and found her as she was walking the dog away from the arena a short time later. His brows drew together in a quizzical stare. 'He didn't win, then?'

'I'm afraid not.'

'He probably cooked his goose when he tried to grab the judge's jacket. He seems to have a thing about flapping edges, doesn't he?'

'It was your idea that I should bring him here,' she retorted. 'He's a beautiful-looking dog, but he'll never win any awards for his behaviour.'

Mark laughed. 'Come and have a drink with me over by the refreshment tent. The caterers have set out tables and chairs, and there's a railing where we can tie Kingston's lead for a while. He can sit and watch us.'

'All right.' She walked with him across the grass. 'It looks as though you're going to collect a tidy sum for the dialysis machine,' she said when they were seated at a table just a short time later. She had a glass of wine and a plate of sandwiches in front of her, and Mark had settled for lager and was helping himself to the sandwiches. Jamie and her father were still wandering around, looking at all the stalls and trying out some of the activities. Kingston was at their feet, tied up to a railing but perfectly happy, scoffing an ice cream.

'It's looking good,' Mark said. 'The sale of raffle tickets has brought in quite a large amount already.'

'Are those the prizes?' she asked, glancing over at a table on a raised dais.

He nodded. 'There are consolation prizes, like baskets of fruit and bottles of wine, but there's also a television set and hi-fi unit. A sponsor has given us the main prize—a holiday. Do you want to wander over there and take a look?'

She nodded. Finishing off her drink, she turned to Kingston. 'You had better stay there,' she said, 'and finish that ice cream. You're making a revolting mess. I'll be back in just a minute.'

Kingston took no notice. His attention had wandered to a cardboard box that someone had left lying around, and he was doing his best to demolish it. Sarah slipped away with Mark. 'I don't really want him anywhere near that stand,' she told Mark. 'He might start getting ideas. It's best to leave him by the railing for the time being, I think. We won't be too far away, so we'll be able to keep an eye on him.'

They went over to the stand, and Mark handed over some notes and bought a wad of raffle tickets. He handed them to her, and she looked at him in astonishment. 'These are for me?'

'What would I do with a basket of fruit?' he said. He slipped an arm around her waist as she glanced at the collection of prizes, and her whole body reacted to the intimacy of his touch. It felt good, and she absorbed the warmth of his hand as it rested on the curve of her hip, sending ripples of tingling sensation to reverberate through her soft flesh and fire up her nervous system. It surprised her, the way she was feeling. She had never felt this way before, and she had never responded to any man in the way she did to Mark.

Lost in thought, she was suddenly alerted to a commotion that was starting up to one side of them, and she looked up in horror to see that Kingston had sneaked up and was intent on lifting a box of chocolates from the display.

'How did he get loose?' she exclaimed. Then she saw Jamie, jumping up and down and squealing with laughter. He started to run towards Kingston, and the dog, realising that he had been rumbled, grabbed the box of chocolates in his mouth and took to his heels.

'Oh, no. Kingston, stop.'

'He runned away,' Jamie shouted gleefully.

Her father said awkwardly, 'I'm sorry about that. I was talking to someone and I didn't realise that Jamie had undone the lead before it was too late.'

'I'll get him,' Mark said, already breaking into a sprint.

Sarah glanced at her father. 'Will you look after Jamie for me?'

He nodded, and she hurried after Mark. The dog, still with the chocolate box firmly gripped between his teeth, was heading towards the flower-beds in the distance, and she hoped that Mark would catch up with him before he reached them.

Kingston flew through the spring flowers without a care in the world, and Mark caught hold of him just as he was about to make a return run. 'Got you,' he said.

'Oh, no, look at that.' Sarah swept her glance over the trampled flowers and was aghast. 'I'm so sorry. What on earth will your parents think? I never dreamt that he would do something like that.' She caught sight of the crumpled box of chocolates. 'And the raffle prize… Kingston, you're a bad dog,' she said, shaking her head. 'Look at what you've done.'

'He actually looks pleased with himself,'

Mark said, laughing. He glanced down at the dog. 'That was a good game, wasn't it?'

Kingston sat down, panting, and Sarah could have sworn that he was grinning.

'I'll have to get my father's car and go to the shops,' she said. 'I'll see if I can find some chocolates to replace those.'

Mark shook his head. 'Don't worry about that. We have another box in the house. Come with me and we'll go and get them.'

By this time her father and Jamie had caught up with them. 'I think I'll take charge of you,' her father said, taking hold of Kingston's lead. 'We'll have no more of this, my lad.'

Kingston seemed to realise that the game was up, and he trotted along beside her father and Jamie, looking somewhat subdued. Jamie thought it was wonderful fun, though, and hopped and danced all the way back to the fair, thoroughly enjoying himself.

'I'll take him to the refreshments tent and sit him down for some lunch,' her father said. 'I expect you're hungry, aren't you, Jamie?'

Jamie nodded. Sarah said, 'I'm just going to go with Mark to get some more chocolates to replace the raffle prize. I shan't be long.'

'Take your time,' her father said. 'We'll be fine.'

Sarah was still worrying about the flower-beds, but she walked with Mark into the house and hoped that they wouldn't come across his parents just yet. She had to work out what she was going to say to them.

'There's a box of chocolates in the bureau in the dining-room,' Mark said. 'Through here.' He led the way, and when they reached the room Sarah stood and looked around, taking in the splendour of her surroundings. Everything about this house was luxurious, and the furniture and soft furnishings were all of the very best quality. The walls were panelled with beautifully carved timber, and there were two oil paintings by famous artists, depicting country landscapes.

Sarah was in awe of everything. She was still staring about her when Mark turned away from the bureau and placed a box of chocolates on a nearby table.

'I don't know how I'm going to explain to your parents,' she told him. 'They must think I'm a dreadful person. I can't even control my dog. I should never have—'

'It's all right,' Mark said, coming towards her. She shook her head. 'No, it isn't.' She waved her arms, gesturing around the room. 'Look at all this… They're used to having everything in its place, in perfect order. And then I come along…'

'I told you, you don't have to worry,' Mark said. By now he was standing in front of her. He slid his arms around her waist.

'That's all right for you to say, you—'

She didn't get to say any more, though, because all at once he was kissing her, effectively cutting off her words. He edged her backwards, pressuring her against the wood panelling, and then he deepened the kiss, crushing the softness of her lips beneath his as though he would possess all of her. He drew the breath from her body and left her gasping, yearning for more.

He kissed her until she was senseless, until every thought had left her head and all that remained was a longing to have him run his hands all over her. Perhaps he read her mind because he did just that, gliding his hands over her curves, stroking her and drawing her up against him so that every part of her was in searing contact with his long body. She melted against him, the strength of his muscled thigh bringing flame to course through her blood. She couldn't get enough of him. What was wrong with her?

'Mark,' she managed, but he was busy trailing kisses over her face, along the curve of her throat, sliding ever downwards until he reached the curve of her breast. She pulled in a ragged breath, and he sighed against the smooth slope of her creamy flesh.

'Sarah,' he muttered huskily, 'do you know that you make me crazy, that you make me lose my mind? I want you… I need you… I can't think straight when you're around. Do you know what you do to me?'

Her lips parted, as though she would answer him, but her head was whirling, and she was finding it hard to take in what he was saying. 'Mark, I…'

She stopped speaking then, and whatever either of them would have said faded into oblivion when they suddenly heard voices coming from nearby.

'What was that?' Sarah whispered. She stiffened, and tried to look around.

Mark reluctantly dragged himself away from her and he, too, gazed around the room. 'It must be the caterers going into the kitchen next door,' he muttered. 'I'd forgotten about them.'

He looked down at her and frowned, as though his head was clearing at last. 'I suppose they could come in here at any moment.' He winced. 'Perhaps we had better go and join the others outside.'

It was just as well that they pulled themselves together, Sarah thought a moment later. Mark's mother met them as they walked out through the dining-room doors and onto the paved terrace outside.

'I've been looking for you,' she said. She

nodded towards Sarah and glanced at Mark. 'Your father's getting ready to draw the raffle.'

Mark showed her the chocolates. 'I went to fetch these,' he said.

Sarah put in quickly, 'It was all my fault. I should never have left Kingston tied up. I might have known something would go wrong. I'll pay for the chocolates, and of course I'll pay for any damage to the garden. Will you let me know how much it will be?'

'I won't hear of it,' his mother said. 'The gardener will soon put things right, and as to the chocolates, you should forget about it.' She turned and walked with them to the dais where the raffle was being held.

Sarah didn't make any more attempts to put things right. She didn't know how to begin, because she realised that Mark's family were above any of that. They lived in a different world to hers.

Mark was roped in to help out with the organisation of events for the rest of the afternoon, and Sarah stayed with Jamie and her father, and tried to ensure that there were no more mishaps. She wondered if Mark was avoiding her.

When they decided it was time to leave an hour or so later, she sought him out to say goodbye to him. He was clearing away some of the litter from around the raffle stall.

'You had a good crowd here today,' her father said.

'We did.' Mark smiled briefly. 'It's been a really successful day, one way or another. We're well on the way to getting the dialysis machine, and the grand opening of the new renal unit's only a couple of weeks away. I'm really pleased with the way things are going.'

He looked at Sarah, but their leave-taking was calm and unemotional. He made no mention of what had happened between them earlier, and Sarah wondered if he was regretting it. She realised that it had been a spur-of-the-moment thing, something that had simply happened and would probably be forgotten.

Not by her, because she had been affected

deeply, more so than had ever happened in her life before, and she had come to realise that she was very much aware of Mark, of wanting him, and needing him.

It was an odd, unaccustomed sensation. Was this love, this strange butterfly feeling in her stomach? Falling for Mark could never come to anything, though, could it? Wanting him to love her in return was just a dream, a whimsical fancy. He had kissed her to shut her up, that was all. With him, it was a purely physical thing. He had never said that he loved her.

It was just a week later, when Sarah was back at work, that preparations for the opening of the new renal unit began to show signs of real progress.

Mark was standing with his father by a table, looking over an architect's model of the hospital. 'I'm really glad that you've managed to find the time to show me around the unit,' his father said. 'Things have gone well and it's all been finished ahead of schedule, hasn't it?'

'It has.' Mark smiled at his father. 'We're going to have the grand opening next week, but I thought you would appreciate a quick preview.' He turned and acknowledged a low-voiced comment from someone who stood next to him.

Sarah watched the group of men from a short distance away. There were about a couple of dozen people all told, and they had all gathered together in a room just along the corridor from A and E. It was a meeting point, and she was there in a public-relations capacity, to serve coffee and to help people feel at ease.

She helped herself to coffee from the filter machine, and Megan came to stand alongside her. 'I always feel uncomfortable at these get-togethers,' Megan said. 'I never feel as though I really fit in. They all seem to be on a different plane to us, don't they?'

'I know what you mean,' Sarah murmured. 'It's probably because they are. I suppose that's why they're called "suits". They look impressive and high profile, as though they spend their lives moving among influential circles. We're more hands-on—workers at the coalface, so to speak.'

Megan chuckled. 'At least you changed out of your scrubs for the occasion.'

Sarah smiled and sipped at her coffee. She saw someone turn to Stuart Ballard, Mark's father, and heard him say, 'We're all very grateful to you for your help with this project. Not just for your generous donation, but also for the tireless work you've done to raise funds in other areas. Without your assistance we wouldn't have been able to get this project off the ground.'

Sarah recognised the man as management. He was one of the smartly dressed executives who had been showing various people around the hospital over the last week. There had been a flurry of activity, and everyone was getting ready for the big event. She hadn't even seen much of Mark. When he wasn't working, he was talking to management.

Today, four of the management team had descended briefly on A and E and were intent on revealing the new unit to Mark's father and to medical personnel from hospitals round about, those that were within the catchment area that would be served by the unit.

Owen was among the group of visitors, and now he murmured something to his companion and slipped away from the crowd.

He came over to Sarah. 'I was hoping I'd get a chance to talk to you before we move on,' he said. He gave her a hug, his arms going around her and holding her close, and when Sarah recovered from the intimacy of the gesture, she looked around and saw that Megan had moved away.

Perhaps she felt that she was intruding. Sarah pressed her lips together and hoped that no one else had seen his exuberant greeting. She sent a surreptitious glance around the room and then wished that she hadn't done that. Mark was watching her, his eyes narrowing on Owen and his gaze fixed on Owen's arm, which was still draped around her. Self-conscious now, she tried to ease herself away from him.

Owen didn't seem to notice her discomfiture. 'You can see why they think so highly of your boss,' he said in a low aside. 'They don't get many people who bring their families along with bulging cheque-books. It must have seemed like a heaven-sent opportunity when Mark introduced his father to them.'

'Don't you think that you might be misjudging him?' Sarah murmured. 'He's wealthy, I grant you, but I've never known Mark to make a big thing of his background. I think he's genuinely pleased that we're getting the renal unit. A lot of people are going to benefit from it.'

Owen's expression was sardonic. 'I can see that you've fallen in with the crowd of worshippers at his feet.'

Sarah wasn't going to rise to his sarcasm. 'It isn't like that. We've needed something like this for a long time, and the whole community has backed the project. The hospital chiefs are bound to be appreciative of any efforts to help.'

'It's a pity they don't concentrate their attention on those things more often,' he said. 'Then we wouldn't have to go along with all the hoohah about targets and waiting times. We all have enough to do, caring for our patients, without worrying about reaching some artificial quota.'

'You could be right,' she said, 'but they're not actually to blame for any of it, are they? They just have to go along with pronouncements from above and then try to compete with hospitals in other regions.' Owen was bound to be feeling cynical. Management had turned him down for the job that Mark had been given.

She was suddenly aware of Mark coming towards them.

'Hello, Owen,' he said. 'I'm glad that you were able to come along to visit our new unit. How's the job going at your hospital? Is it what you expected it to be?'

'It's excellent,' Owen said. 'Things are running very smoothly, though we could always do with more staff, of course.'

Mark nodded. 'I'd heard something of the sort. I hope you're not thinking of trying to take Sarah away from us. She still has a contract here, you know.'

Owen glanced at Sarah, and then turned back once more to Mark. 'I know that. If I hoped to persuade her, it wasn't A and E that I had in mind. She's always been very good in paediatric medicine. I think if she was to specialise in that area, she could go far.'

'That's probably true, but I hope that she'll stay here. We're crying out for A and E staff.'

Sarah glowered at both of them and put in tersely, 'I hope you two haven't forgotten that I'm standing here. You're talking about me as though I have no say in the matter.'

Mark made a wry smile. 'You're right, of course. I'm sorry about that.' He gave Owen a long look. 'I'm sure you know that we would have valued your services here, if you had stayed.'

Owen sent him a disparaging stare. 'You must know that I would never have done that.'

Mark shrugged. 'It was your choice.' He glanced towards the management team. 'I think they're getting ready to move on,' he murmured. 'I have to go and join them.'

Sarah followed the direction of his gaze and watched him as he moved away. 'I must go back to work,' she told Owen. 'We're going to be short-handed while Mark is away for the next hour.'

Owen lifted a brow. 'Isn't this his day off? Is he taking time off in the middle of a shift?'

She shook her head. 'An occasional bit of PR is part of his job. Anyway, his bleeper's on. He'll stay in touch in case he's needed.'

Owen straightened and looked at her searchingly. 'I'll probably be able to come back and see you before I go,' he said. 'Would you like to have dinner with me this evening?'

'I can't. I have to stay with Jamie. My father looks after him whenever he can, when he's not on call or taking surgery, but I need to be there this evening.'

'Some other time, perhaps?'

'Maybe.' She was noncommittal and he moved away, frowning, and went to join the rest of the visitors who were trooping out into the corridor.

Sarah went back to work, and almost straight away she was plunged into dealing with one crisis after another. She'd hardly had time to pause for breath when the triage nurse hurried over to her.

'Would you come and take a look at this patient for me?' Megan asked. 'She's complaining of abdominal pain, along with diarrhoea and vomiting. It could be just a simple abdominal complaint, but she looks very ill and I'm concerned about her condition. Do you mind? I know that you're busy.'

'No, I don't mind at all.' Sarah went along with Megan to the treatment room.

The woman did look in a bad way, and when Sarah checked her over she was disturbed to find that her patient's heart was racing at around three times what was normal and that she was feverish. She was near to collapse and showed signs of tremor and extreme agitation.

'I think we'd better cool her down,' Sarah said. 'We'll try sponging her with tepid water and set up some fans in here.' She frowned. 'I haven't quite come across anything like this before.' She wished that Mark was here to advise her, but she didn't want to disturb him while he was with the visitors, and her immediate superior had his hands full right then, dealing with someone who had been brought in from a road traffic accident.

Sarah stopped to think for a moment. 'I'm going to order some blood tests,' she said finally. 'I'll write out the forms for you. We'll need urea and electrolytes, blood glucose and a full blood count, among others. We'd better screen for infection, too.'

'I'll set that up now,' Megan said. Seeing Sarah hesitate, she added, 'Was there anything else?'

'No, that's it for now. I need to check up on her records, to see if there's anything that I'm missing, but when I've done that I'll come and find you.'

'OK.'

Sarah went off to check the computer, and then made a call to the woman's general practitioner. She discovered that her patient, Jane, had a history of thyroid problems. As soon as she had noted down all the details, Sarah hurried back to the treatment room.

Megan said, 'She's getting worse. She's been vomiting again. I think she could be dehydrated.'

'You're probably right. We'll give her IV fluids and saline. I'm going to need thyroid function tests as well.'

'Do you think this is a thyroid problem?' Megan queried. 'I was thinking she had food poisoning.'

'I can't be certain, without doing all the tests, but her GP says there's a history of thyroid problems, and I'm worried about the tremor and her recent weight loss. I think she could be suffering a thyrotoxic crisis.'

'That's rare, isn't it? What would have brought that on?'

'It could have been a number of things—an infection of some sort, emotional stress, or even some kind of trauma. She hasn't had surgery recently, so I can rule that out. The blood tests will give us some of the answers. In the meantime, we'll give her propranolol to bring her heart rate down, and antibiotics to control any infection.'

'Are you not going to wait for the results of the blood tests before giving the antibiotics?'

Sarah shook her head. 'I don't think so. She looks very ill and we need to do everything that we can for her. I don't want to leave anything to chance.' Once again, she wished that Mark was here to advise her one way or the other, but he wouldn't be pleased to be dragged away if the patient turned out to be suffering from nothing more than a simple abdominal complaint, would he?

It was some time later before the results of the tests came through, but they confirmed Sarah's fears. She asked Megan, 'How is she doing?'

'She seems a little calmer now. I think the fluids are helping. She's cooler, and her pulse isn't racing quite so much, but she still seems to be in a bad way.'

'That's more or less what I expected,' Sarah said, nodding. 'I'm going to give her dexamethasone to support her through this, and carbimazole to reduce the level of thyroid hormone. Then we need to refer her for admission.'

Sarah stayed with her patient for a while, until she was satisfied that Jane was beginning to respond to the treatment. Then she told Megan, 'I'm going to take a break, but if you need me for any reason, you can bleep me. 'I'm going up to look in on Ryan for a little while, and then I'll go and see my sister. She wants to know how he is doing. Will you stay here and keep an eye on Jane?'

Megan nodded. 'Don't worry, I'll stay with her, and I'll let you know if there's any problem.'

'Thanks, Megan.'

Sarah hurried away, and went to look in on Ryan.

'There's been no meaningful response,' the nurse said. 'He moved a finger slightly yesterday, but it was a non-directed movement and, as you know, you get these sorts of reactions from time to time. The same thing happened a few days ago.'

Sarah understood what she was saying. Recovery was a long process, and coma patients often exhibited occasional movement or even managed to make some kind of response, but it didn't mean that they were going to suddenly sit up and start talking.

She stayed with Ryan for a few minutes. He was perfectly still, and his eyes were closed, but she talked to him about Hannah and Jamie, and told him that Jamie had made him a clay pot at school.

'It's a bit lopsided, and it wobbles because it's not quite flat at the base, but he's painted it a lovely bright yellow colour. He said he did that for you because you like sunshine yellow, and he thinks you'll be able to put bits and pieces in it. It's sitting on my kitchen window-sill, and Jamie's longing for you to be well enough to come home so that he can give it to you.'

She sat with him for a little while longer, and then told him that she was going to see Hannah.

'Hannah wants to know how you are. I wish that I could tell her that you were awake and asking for her.'

He didn't move, or show any kind of reaction, and she looked at him for a second or two, feeling sad, and guilty because she hadn't been able to do anything for him.

She went to find Hannah, and there at least there was some good news. The nurse said, 'We think that she may not have been as badly injured as we first believed. Now that her acute injury has begun to heal, she's beginning to recover some of her reflexes. Nothing major at the moment, but there is hope.'

'That's wonderful news.' Sarah felt a surge of relief overwhelm her.

'I thought you would be pleased. Hannah's still quite depressed, though, so you should be prepared for that. She hasn't reacted as we hoped she would, but it's not unusual for patients in her condition to be anxious and disheartened. She still has quite a road ahead of her, with physiotherapy and so on.'

'I know, but this news means that at least there's a chance that she's going to walk again, doesn't it?'

'That's true. I've told her the good news, but I'm not sure that she's taken everything in just yet.'

Sarah went and sat with Hannah and talked to her about the results of the tests. 'I know there's nothing too specific just now, but it is good news.'

Hannah was doubtful, as though she was afraid to take too much on trust.

'I don't understand why it has taken so long for the doctors to find out what the damage was,' she said. 'How can I believe them when they say that I might start to get the feeling back in my legs? I still feel pretty much the same as I did when I first came here. Aren't they just trying to make me feel better? They've been doing everything they could to jolly me up from the moment I was admitted here. That's their job, isn't it—to keep encouraging the patient?'

'I think that they're being honest with you,'

Sarah said. 'There was a reason why they couldn't see straight away what damage had been done. When you injured your spine, there was some bleeding and an accumulation of fluid around the spinal cord. That had the effect of compressing your spinal cord and bruising you very badly, and when the spinal cord is affected in that way it can be a lot more serious than if you just bruised an arm or a leg, for instance. Once you start to heal up and the swelling recedes, you can start to recover some of the functions that you had before. From the sound of things, you've been very lucky.'

Hannah stared at her. 'How can you say that I've been lucky? I'm lying here, unable to move, unable to go home and play with my little boy, and as if all that wasn't bad enough, his father is in a coma with no sign of recovery. He was in such a bad way that they didn't even tell me that for a couple of days, or let me see him. How am I supposed to trust anyone?'

Sarah gently touched her sister's hand. 'I know that things seem bad just now, but he is recovering from his other injuries, and there's always the possibility that he will come out of the coma one day.'

Hannah drew her hand away, and her gaze was cold. 'Will he? We can't be sure of anything, can we? Why is he in a coma, anyway? He was conscious and able to talk to you when you found him, wasn't he? The nurse told me that he asked about me when the paramedic first went to him. He wanted to know that I was all right.'

'That's true.' Sarah frowned. 'We didn't know the extent of his injuries to begin with. He had a bang to his head, but he was also bleeding into his chest, and that turned out to be very serious. That's why he lost consciousness.'

'It's the head injury that has put him into a coma, though, isn't it? His neurologist told me that he had a blood clot inside his skull. That's what caused the damage. Isn't that right?'

'Yes, that's true. The surgeon removed it when he was in the operating Theatre.'

'Shouldn't you have noticed that earlier? You could have done something about it, couldn't you? He's being given medication to help counteract the swelling on his brain, but if he'd had that medication earlier, or if you had taken more notice of his head injury from the beginning, he might be up and about now, mightn't he?' Hannah looked at Sarah as though she hated her. 'As it is, he could be brain-damaged. How is Jamie going to understand it if his father doesn't recognise him, or if he isn't the same as he once was?'

Sarah froze. Did Hannah really think that she should have done something more? Her lips were suddenly as dry as dust and her heart was pounding, thudding against her chest wall as though it, too, would punish her.

She said huskily, 'I did what I could for him, Hannah. I did everything possible, you must believe me.'

'It wasn't enough, though, was it? You should have saved him, but you didn't, and perhaps that's because you didn't know how. You said yourself that you weren't sure that you were good enough to work in emergency medicine.'

Hannah's mouth tightened. 'We were going to make a fresh start, Ryan and me. He was going to change—he wasn't going to drink any more, he promised me, and he was going to be a proper father to Jamie. Now everything has gone wrong, hasn't it?'

'I'm sorry. I'm so sorry, Hannah.' Sarah felt wretched. She had hoped that Hannah would feel better when she was given the news that she might walk again. She hadn't expected to have all this bitter recrimination showered on her, and now she felt as though she had been slapped. Her own sister despised her, and that felt like a lead weight bearing down on her.

'I'm tired,' Hannah said. 'I want to sleep now.' She closed her eyes, and when Sarah tried to speak to her, she didn't answer.

After a few minutes Sarah stood up and quietly left the room. She went back down to A and E, but she felt as though she was in a trance, as though the floor had shifted from beneath her feet and she was feeling her way.

Owen was back from the tour of the renal

unit, and he stopped and spoke to her for a while, but she answered him in bleak monosyllables until he asked, 'How is your sister? Megan told me that you had gone to see her. Is she still unable to walk? I thought there might be some good news by now.'

'The injury still has to heal. It will take time, but hopefully the damage isn't as bad as it seemed.'

'That's good, isn't it?' He glanced at her, his gaze serious. 'Is Ryan still in the same condition?'

'He's still in a coma.'

'I'm sorry.' He frowned. 'I can see that you don't feel like talking. It must be upsetting for you.' He looked uncertain as to what to do next, but then he said, 'I think I should go now. Perhaps I could call you later in the week?'

She nodded, and he walked away. She watched him leave the room, and then she went over to the desk and picked up a chart. Perhaps work would help in some small way to blot out Hannah's harsh words.

'Is something wrong?'

She looked up, and saw that Mark had come to stand alongside her. 'No. I just have to check up on a patient.'

He looked at her oddly. 'I see that Owen has just left. It must be difficult for you to get used to the idea of him going away again when you were once colleagues—more than that, in fact.'

'Yes, I suppose it is. I was so used to working with him, and now it seems strange to have him come to visit.' She looked away and tried to concentrate on the chart. 'I see that you have signed off on my thyroid patient. I take it that she's been admitted?'

'Yes, she was taken to the ward while you were away.' He looked at her searchingly. 'You should have called for me, you know. These cases are unusual, and there's always a chance that the patient might not survive.'

She sent him a worried glance. 'Do you mean that my patient might not survive? I did what I could for her.'

He shook his head. 'No, I mean in general.

Next time that you're uncertain in any way, you should call me.'

'I'll do that.' Her hand had begun to shake, and she closed it into a fist so that the tremors would not show. Did he, too, doubt her ability? She had hoped that he would come to have some trust in her and that they might grow closer to one another after what had happened between them at his father's house, but he had made no mention of it since then, and she had tried to accept that she was expecting too much.

He didn't even respect her as a doctor and she didn't see how else she fitted into his life-style. Given his family background, there would have to be a strong reason for him to want to take things further with her, and she couldn't see that happening. There was no future for her with him, was there?

All at once she felt helpless, out of her depth. Why was she clinging on to the hope that she might some day be good at emergency work? Perhaps she would do better to consider Owen's offer of a job.

CHAPTER SEVEN

'I'VE been thinking things over, as I said I would,' Sarah murmured, frowning as she took the phone call. She wasn't sure why Owen wanted to talk to her while she was at work, but perhaps he was in his office and had taken the first opportunity during a break. 'It's difficult for me, because there are still around six weeks left on my contract here.'

'Why don't you come over to my hospital and just take a look at the paediatric unit?' Owen said. 'You know that you've never been too sure about emergency work, and you could at least just come for a visit. It might help you to make up your mind, one way or the other. I'm not going to pressure you, but the interviews are going to start soon, and if you were to decide that you want to work in paediatrics after all, it would be a shame to miss out on the chance.'

'You're probably right,' Sarah answered. 'Perhaps I'll do that.' She was thoughtful for a moment. 'I suppose I could drive over there on Thursday. It fits in with my day off, and Jamie will be at school, so there should be no problem with that.'

She replaced the receiver a moment later and then stood for a while, wondering whether she had made the right decision. Mark came over and found some laboratory forms from a box on the desk, and as he glanced through them and wrote his signature on a couple, he threw her a quick look.

'Was that Owen? I heard that he'd tried to call you earlier today when you were busy with a patient. He's very keen to get you on his side, isn't he?'

'I think he's proud of his work at the hospital. He's very impressed with the paediatric unit there, and he won't be happy until I've been over and taken a look at it.'

'He doesn't work in the paediatric unit.'

'That's true, but he wants to set up something similar alongside A and E. I suppose that's why he keeps an eye on things there.'

'So you'll be going over there this week?' When she nodded, he said, 'You'll have to let me know how you get on.'

She was disappointed by his level tone, and maybe that was because she was hoping for a different kind of reaction from him. He wasn't trying to dissuade her, and that was a little odd, but perhaps he didn't really care whether she stayed or went. He knew that her contract was coming to an end, but he wasn't trying to influence her either way. He probably already had someone in mind for her job, if she should decide to leave.

'I'll do that.' She glanced through some notes she had made, trying to keep her mind on her job, but she was finding it difficult to concentrate while Mark was watching her.

She wanted so much to be able to turn to him and be at ease with him, but since that day at his father's house nothing had been quite the same. Perhaps, after the dog had run amok and his parents had seen the full extent of the damage to the flower-beds, he had realised that they had nothing in common. His parents had been polite and civil towards her, but it must have been plain to see that she simply wouldn't fit in with his way of life.

He said, 'I heard that Hannah was having physiotherapy. How is she getting on?'

'All right. It's a slow business, but at least she's co-operating with everyone. She wants to be able to go home to be with little Jamie.'

'That's understandable. I suppose that as she begins to feel stronger some of her depression will lift.'

Sarah looked up at him in surprise. 'I didn't know that you'd heard about that.'

He nodded. 'I spoke with one of the nurses. I suppose I feel involved, since we were there at the scene of the accident... And she's your sister, of course. That makes me concerned for her, on your behalf.'

He hesitated, then added, 'I imagine a lot of her depression must stem from the fact that Ryan is still incapacitated. It seems odd that she had to run away from him and come to you, and yet now she's feeling that she has to blame someone for his condition.'

He was looking at her cautiously, and Sarah realised that somehow he must have put two and two together. He must know that Hannah blamed her for what had happened. She still went to visit her sister, but their meetings were fraught with tension. Hannah was not giving way.

'She told me that they had talked things through on the day of the accident, and they were hoping to get together again. I think she always loved him, deep down, but he was a different man when he had been drinking. He promised her that he would stop.'

'Is that likely? Or rather, would he have been likely to do that if he hadn't been involved in the accident?'

'I don't know. Perhaps he had some issues that he needed to resolve, and he may have turned to drink to try to avoid them. I suppose it's always possible that Hannah had managed to persuade him to have some kind of counselling. I don't think she would have simply taken his word for it that he would stop. I know Hannah, and she would have expected some kind of commitment from him that he was determined to change his way of going on.'

He said, 'You've been going to see Ryan, haven't you? I think that's a good idea, to keep talking to him. The nurses have been wheeling Hannah along there as well. There is a school of thought that if you keep trying to stimulate someone who is in a coma you might eventually get some response.'

'Yes, I've been trying that. There hasn't been much change in his condition up to now—just the occasional twitch of a finger, and a couple of times he actually opened his eyes, but then he reverted to his usual stillness. I left some tapes with the nurses so that they can play them for him when we're not able to visit. Mostly they're tapes of Jamie talking to Kingston, or tapes of Jamie playing with his friends. The nursery school is planning a visit to the seaside soon, a day trip, and I managed to get a tape of the children talking about it.' She frowned. 'I don't know what else to do.'

He touched her hand, covering her fingers with his palm. 'You're doing what you can,' he said. 'You should stop punishing yourself. You can't do any more.'

'I know.' The gentle compassion in the way he laid his hand on hers was meant to be reassuring, but it was almost her undoing. It was the first real contact she'd had with him since that day he had kissed her, and it brought home to her how much she had missed that closeness.

He released her and moved away as the desk clerk finished checking the computer and came back to the reception area. Sarah took her notes with her and went in search of her patient.

The visit to the paediatric unit at Owen's hospital went off well enough. The doctors and nurses who staffed the department were friendly and welcoming, and Sarah knew that if she chose to work in this hospital she would be able to settle in without too many problems.

Owen was eager to show her around, and when he was due for a break they went to the cafeteria and had lunch together. 'What did you think?' he asked. 'Could you see yourself working here?'

'Possibly,' she said. 'I would need to give it some serious thought.'

'Are you still thinking of working in A and E when your contract finishes?'

'I haven't made up my mind yet. Ever since my mother died I've wanted to work in Emergency, and I believed that anything else would be second best for me. I just need to think it through and get it clear in my head. There are so many reasons for and against.'

Owen gave her a considering look. 'How far does Mark figure in your reasoning? Can you see yourself moving away from him?'

'Why do you ask that?'

He gave a crooked smile. 'Because I think

you care about him. You leap to his defence and you admire the way he runs things, and besides all that I've seen the way you look at him when you think no one's watching. I doubt that you've even let him know how you feel.'

'I think my decisions will be based more on how things are with my family,' she said, side-stepping the issue. 'Hannah is beginning to respond to physiotherapy, but she'll need help with Jamie for a long time to come. I might possibly be able to persuade her to move with me, and I could arrange home care for her, but neither of us would want to be too far away from my father. We would have to be within visiting distance of him and Ryan.'

'I don't see that as a problem. It's a two-hour drive to get here from where you are now, but you could find somewhere to live around the halfway point.'

'Maybe. I'll have to think about it.' There was always the possibility that she could find a position in a hospital nearer home.

He didn't push her any more, and Sarah made the drive back home, her head filled with uncertainties.

The next day she went back to work in A and E. Mark sent a swift glance her way when she arrived in the department, but he was busy with a patient and he said briefly, 'You made the tour of the paediatric unit, then?'

She nodded. 'It was impressive. The facilities there are wonderful.'

He made a disgruntled sound in the back of his throat, and then turned his attention back to his patient. Sarah went and got on with her work, and didn't see much of him throughout the rest of the day. He seemed to be continuously on the move, constantly under pressure. Perhaps that was because there was a major influx of trauma patients.

Towards the end of her shift, he called out to her as he was working on an injured man, applying pressure to a wound as the patient was being wheeled on a trolley bed towards the treatment room.

'There's a woman coming in by ambulance. She's an asthmatic and she's thirty-five weeks pregnant. Will you take her? Get Jonathan to help you. I'm going to have to try and get my patient up to surgery. I can't leave him.'

'Yes, of course.' She could see that Mark was trying to stem bleeding and they were pumping blood into the patient as fast as they could. There was no way that Mark was going to be able to help her.

When the paramedics brought the woman in, she was suffering an asthma attack and was being given nebulised salbutamol. It was clear to see that she was heavily pregnant.

Sarah started to examine her, but the next moment Megan said, 'We're losing her.'

Sarah quickly gave the patient a shot of epinephrine, but after a minute or two Megan said, 'I can't find a pulse. She's stopped breathing.'

'I'm going to intubate,' Sarah said. 'We need to get the obstetrician and the paediatrician down here.' A nurse hurried away to make the call, and Sarah started the intubation.

She introduced the point of the curved laryn-goscope blade into the epiglottic fold until she could see the inlet of the larynx. Then she passed the endotracheal tube into the trachea, removed the laryngoscope, inflated the cuff and fixed the tube in place with tape.

'All right, I've secured the airway. Let's get her on oxygen, and we need to get her into a left lateral tilt position. We'll support her with pillows to keep her propped on her side.'

'Why are we doing that?' Jonathan asked with a frown.

'It helps with the flow of blood, and it should make chest compressions more successful in providing sufficient cardiac output.'

Megan took over with the oxygen, and Sarah began chest compressions, but after a few minutes she said, 'I need to defibrillate.' Quickly, she put gel on the patient's chest, slapped gel pads on and then placed the defi-brillator paddles there in order to shock the heart.

They worked as a team for several minutes,

trying to resuscitate the woman, and eventually Sarah said, 'How is the foetus doing?'

Jonathan said, 'It's struggling. The heart rate is falling dangerously low.'

'We're going to have to do an emergency Caesarean. Is there a Theatre ready?'

Megan shook her head. 'No, I already checked.'

'We can't wait. Where are the obstetrician and the paediatrician? I called for them ages ago.'

'They're run off their feet upstairs,' Jonathan said. 'They're dealing with a breech presentation and a woman who is haemorrhaging. They said they would get down here as soon as possible.'

Sarah was worried. She was exhausted after a long day, and she wasn't at all sure that she could handle this on her own, but there was no one else around who could help out. She was certain that this woman needed expert help. With the foetus struggling to survive, there were two patients who needed help, not just the one.

She pulled in a deep breath. 'OK, let's prepare her for a Caesarean section.'

She made a midline skin incision, and then

incised the underlying uterus. Working as quickly as she could, she delivered the baby, holding it head down and below the level of the mother's abdomen. Jonathan clamped and cut the umbilical cord.

'The baby's not breathing,' he said. 'There's no heartbeat.'

Sarah could see that the baby was limp, with no reflexes, and his colour was bluish. 'Start resuscitation. I have to look after the mother. I can't leave her.'

Jonathan blanched, but he turned away and began resuscitation. Just then the doors of the treatment room flew open and the obstetrician arrived, with the paediatrician following close on her heels.

'We'll take things from here,' the obstetrician said. Sarah moved back to give her room.

The baby still wasn't making a sound, and Sarah was dreadfully afraid that she had been too late. A delay of just a few minutes could have made for a bad outcome, and she was desperately worried that she had waited too long.

'We're going to have to get both of these patients to Intensive Care,' the obstetrician said after a few minutes. 'We'll keep the mother on the heart monitor and IV fluids. I'm concerned about her breathing problems and the blood loss, and her blood pressure is falling.'

Mother and child were wheeled away at top speed, and Sarah was left in the treatment room, staring at the empty space where the trolley had been. Megan and the other nurse had gone with the patients, and Jonathan was looking worriedly after the disappearing baby.

'I think perhaps he was starting to breathe,' he said. 'I can't be sure…but there's a chance that he'll be all right, isn't there?' He was frowning, looking doubtful, looking to her for reassurance, and Sarah nodded, unwilling to show him her fears. He was a junior doctor and he had done everything that he could. She was the one who was to blame if anything had gone wrong.

'Go and take a break,' she said. 'You did well. You did everything you could.'

He looked thankful to escape, and Sarah was glad to be left alone. When the door shut behind him the enormity of what had happened washed over her and she started to cry, soft, silent tears that trickled down her cheeks so that she tasted the salt of them on her lips.

'What happened?' Mark came into the room and looked at her questioningly.

She stared up at him, not speaking, startled because she hadn't heard the door open. Then she said, her voice choked, 'The mother went into cardiac arrest. The baby wasn't breathing, and there was no pulse. I tried…I tried to save them, but I waited too long. I failed them both.'

'Where are they now?'

She dashed the tears away from her face. 'They've been taken to Intensive Care.' She struggled to stop her mouth from trembling, the troubles of the whole unhappy day falling around her.

'I'm no good at this,' she whispered. 'I thought I could make a go of it, but it's hopeless. I'll never make an emergency doctor, will I? I don't think quickly enough, I don't act quickly enough, and I'm scared all the time. I just can't make it.'

He stared at her, and he didn't speak for a long moment. Then he said, 'You're probably right. You've always been doubtful about your abilities, and it's most likely true. You're not cut out for this type of work. No matter how hard you try, you just can't do it. You might as well give up.'

Her lips parted in shock. His expression was grim, his mouth a hard line, and he wasn't pulling any punches. For the first time since she had begun to work with him, he was telling it how it really was, without giving her any leeway or any excuses. He was telling her what he really thought.

He said, 'Perhaps you should go away for a while. Go away for the weekend, maybe, and take some time to think things through. You'll need to consider where you go from here when your contract finishes in a few weeks. Perhaps you'd do better in research or something along those lines…something where you don't have to deal with patients directly.'

She didn't know what to say. She was still in shock from what had happened and she hadn't expected to hear such harsh words from him. He was telling her to go away, and that wouldn't involve simply leaving the hospital. It would take her away from him, too.

He was right, though. She needed to go away, to think about where her future lay. And whatever she decided, it wasn't likely that he would want her, was it? He needed to be with someone he could respect, someone he could care for and feel good about, but it wasn't going to be her. She didn't stand a chance.

He despised her for her weakness, for her inability to do the job. Why had she ever thought she could make a go of things?

CHAPTER EIGHT

SARAH looked through the door into the intensive care unit. What was happening to the mother and her baby in there? She was desperate to know that all was well, and she started to push at the door, about to go in. Then she stopped. Her fingers were trembling.

How could she cope if she discovered that things had gone even further downhill after they had left the treatment room just a short time ago? She wasn't ready to face any more bad news right now. Slowly she turned away, and saw that Jonathan was approaching.

'Have you been in to see them?' he asked, looking worried. 'Have they managed to pull through?'

'I don't know,' she said. 'I've just remembered that I have to go somewhere. I'll come back later.'

He nodded, and after a moment's hesitation he pushed open the door and went in. Sarah started to hurry away.

She almost collided with Mark. He was making his way along the corridor towards her, and there was no way of avoiding him. He said, 'You've not been in to see them, have you?'

'No, I haven't. I just realised that I have to go and meet my dad and Jamie. They're coming in to see Ryan and Hannah.'

'Of course they are.' He looked at her, frowning. 'You're off duty this weekend, aren't you? Will you manage to get some time to yourself?'

She nodded. 'Jamie's going on a school outing tomorrow, a day trip to the seaside. I think my dad's going to go with him.' She straightened and looked him in the eye. 'It will give me time to do as you suggested. I'll be able to think through what I need to do.'

'You'll let me know what you decide on

Monday? I'd like to be able to get on with sorting out our staffing situation for when your contract finishes. We're going to advertise the position as a permanent staff grade. I want to iron things out ahead of time, so that we can have a fluid handover.'

Her breath caught in her throat. He didn't care, did he? He didn't have any deep feelings for her, or how could he treat her this way? 'Yes. I'll do that. I'll make my decision this weekend.'

He inclined his head briefly, and then he moved away from her and headed towards the intensive care unit. She stared after him. She didn't know him like this. He was cold towards her, rigid, uncompromising in his manner. It was upsetting, and she hurried away, going in search of her father.

'Are you sure that you won't come with us?' her father asked her the next day. 'I'm sure that we could find room for you on the coach.'

Sarah shook her head. 'There won't be any room. The teachers told me that the coach was fully booked and, anyway, I really need to be on my own to think things through.'

He looked at her sadly. 'What will you do? Will you stay here? I'm worried about you, Sarah. I don't like to leave you like this. I've never seen you this uncertain and lost.'

She tried a smile. 'I'll be all right. I think I'll go to the little cove where Hannah and I used to go when we were very young. Do you remember it? We went there lots of times, didn't we? Mum used to love it, and we would climb on the rocks, and you and Mum were forever telling us to be careful.'

'I remember. You must have been about fifteen the last time we went there. It was the year before your mother died, wasn't it?'

'That's right. I think I'll go there today and just sit quietly for a while and take in the sea breeze. It'll only take me about half an hour to get there, won't it? Don't worry about me. I'll be fine.'

She kissed him on the cheek, and then turned and gave Jamie a big hug. 'You go and have a lovely time, Jamie,' she said.

'I'll bring you some shells,' he promised. 'You like shells, don't you?'

'I do. That will be lovely.'

It was an hour or so later when she finally set off for the cove. The weather was warm and the sun was shining, but as she discovered the little stretch of beach once more and went to sit on a flat rock looking out to sea, she felt strangely chilled. There were only a few people there, and they were sitting, enjoying a picnic lunch and quietly relaxing in the sunshine. She felt out of place.

Years ago, she recalled, this cove had rung with laughter as she and Hannah had chased each other along the sand, but now the silence was marked. She felt the loss of her family keenly. Hannah was angry with her because she had failed her, and her mother was gone.

Her mother had been the impetus for her turning to medicine. It had been because of her that she'd wanted so much to succeed. Working in A and E had been her goal—it had been what she wanted to do more than anything—

and now her dream had turned to ashes. She wasn't any good at emergency work.

She stayed at the cove for a while, thinking about everything that had gone wrong, and then she decided to stretch her legs and walk across the beach and up onto the clifftop.

She had lunch at a little café, and then wandered around until she came across a grassed area where children were playing, with their mothers looking on. There was a bench seat in the shade of a tree, and she sat down and listened to the shouts of laughter as the children called to one another.

She let her gaze drift around. There was a shallow duckpond to one side, and grassy hillocks with pathways curving this way and that among them.

Some of the children were riding on bikes or tricycles, pedalling along the pathways, laughing and shouting.

'Keep away from the water,' one mother shouted.

'Slow down, Tom,' another called out.

Sarah's glance went to Tom. He was around the same age as Jamie, perhaps a year younger, which would put him at three years old, she guessed. He had fair hair and blue eyes and he was having a great time, pedalling energetically along the narrow path.

Just then she saw another boy riding his bike with equal fervour, hurtling from the opposite direction, and Sarah's heart was suddenly in her mouth. They were going to crash into each other. There was no room on the path for them to pass, and neither of them was applying his brakes.

At the last minute, though, Tom swerved to avoid the boy, and then he seemed to lose control of his tricycle. The bike jolted off the path and raced down the hill, heading straight for the duckpond, with Tom gripping onto the handlebars as though his life depended on it.

Sarah jumped to her feet. She didn't see how he could avoid toppling over and into the duckpond, but she was too far away, and she knew that she wouldn't get to him in time. His mother ran down the slope towards him at an angle, but she wasn't close enough either and there wasn't time for her to grab the bike. 'Use your brakes,' the mother shouted, but the boy was clinging on desperately as though he was afraid to unlock his grip.

Sarah was running, desperate to get to him, but then his mother threw herself sideways, in front of the bike. It crashed into her knee, and the little boy came flying off it and landed half on the grass and half on the pathway bordering the pond.

Mother and son lay there, winded. Sarah went first to the little boy. He sat up shakily and started to cry. 'I banged my head,' he said.

Sarah looked at him. There was a nasty graze on his forehead and it was bleeding, but at least he was sitting up and talking. She took a clean tissue from the pocket of her jeans. 'Here,' she said handing it to him. 'Hold this against your head. Just there, like this,' she said, helping him.

She turned her attention to his mother. She could see some blood trickling down her leg. 'Have you hurt your knee?' she asked.

The woman was sitting up now and she reached out to cuddle her son, comforting him, but now she looked down at her leg. She was wearing a skirt that came down just below her knee, and she lifted the hem a little and checked the damage.

'No, it's not my knee—I think it's my leg,' she muttered. 'There's a cut. I think it's all right, but it's bleeding quite a bit.' She looked up at Sarah. 'You don't have another tissue on you, do you?'

'Yes. Here you are.' Sarah inspected the wound. She frowned and said, 'Actually, this looks like quite a deep cut. I think you probably need a stitch or two in there.'

The woman grimaced. 'Do you think so? It is bleeding a lot, isn't it? I think I caught it on the bike, and then I banged it on the pavement. But I'm more worried about Tom.' She looked at him, and the little boy was gulping back sobs, holding the tissue to his forehead. 'He took a nasty knock on his head.' She lifted the tissue slightly and inspected her son's wound.

She kept her voice low so as not to worry the boy, but she looked at Sarah anxiously. 'It's beginning to come up in a lump. Perhaps I ought to take him along to the hospital.'

Her face crumpled. 'It's all my fault. He was bound to come off his bike when I ran into him, but I didn't know what else to do. I had visions of him somersaulting into the duckpond and banging his head on the concrete floor. I was convinced that he would drown if I didn't get to him in time. And now look—I've hurt him anyway.'

'I don't think you need to worry too much,' Sarah said. 'I'm a doctor,' she explained. 'From the look of him, the damage isn't too bad, but it might be a good idea for them to check him out at the hospital in case there's any delayed concussion.' She paused. 'I'm really more concerned about your leg. I think the wound needs cleaning up, and it ought to be sutured so that it heals properly.'

The woman frowned. 'I'm not worried about myself, but I'd like someone to look Tom over.

It's just that I don't have the car today. We walked here.' She chewed at her lip. 'I suppose I could get a friend to take me.'

Sarah could see that she was shaken up. 'I could take you both to the hospital, if you like. My car's not too far away, and it shouldn't take me too long to run back and get it. We could put the tricycle in the boot.'

The woman looked relieved. 'Would you?' she said.

Sarah nodded. 'You stay here while I go and get my car. I shouldn't be more than a couple of minutes. Try to keep the wad of tissue pressed firmly against the cut, and hold onto Tom so that he doesn't fall back if he should happen to feel dizzy.'

She left them, and returned as she had promised. She lifted the little boy, supporting him with one arm, while she trundled the bike with the other. When they were all safely seated in her car, she set off for the hospital.

Tom vomited when they reached the hospital, and Sarah couldn't be sure whether it was the result of the head injury or whether it had been the ride in the car that had caused the vomiting.

The woman, who told Sarah that her name was Jenny, was upset. 'I should have found some other way to save him,' she said. 'I practically knocked him off the bike. That's why he went flying through the air.'

'He only took a bit of a tumble,' Sarah said. 'It seems worse to you because you were so worried about him, and you reacted instinctively. I don't see what else you could have done. If you hadn't thrown yourself in front of him, he would certainly have ended up in the pond. As you said, he might have ended up hurting himself quite badly in that case. I don't think you have any reason to blame yourself.'

'Do you really think so?'

'I saw what happened,' Sarah said, 'and, yes, I do really think so.'

Sarah helped the woman and the little boy into A and E, and left them in the hands of the doctors and nurses who were on duty. They were attended to fairly quickly, and Jenny said, when she came out of the treatment room, 'I've rung my husband. He's going to come over and pick us up, so you don't need to wait around for us any longer. Thank you so much for your help. I'm really grateful to you for everything that you've done.'

'That's all right. I'm glad that I was able to do something.' Sarah smiled. 'Have they stitched the wound up for you?'

Jenny nodded. 'That nice doctor—Dr Ballard, I think he said his name was—he came and looked at me, and told me that Tom is going to be all right. He told me what to look out for when we leave here, and he said that we can give him infant paracetamol if he needs it. I just have to wait around now for a nurse to come and give me a tetanus shot, and then we can go home.'

Sarah stiffened at the mention of Mark's name, but she said gently enough, 'That's good. I'm glad that everything turned out all right for you. I'll leave Tom's tricycle at the reception desk for you.'

She said goodbye to both of them, and wondered if she would manage to get away from A and E without bumping into Mark. She hadn't realised that he was on duty today.

She left the bike, as promised, and she had reached as far as the corridor outside A and E, when he came after her. 'I heard about your rescue mission,' he said dryly. 'I thought you were supposed to be taking some time to think things through? It looks as though you managed to avoid the issue instead.'

She looked at him, and her chin lifted. 'I have thought things through,' she murmured.

He lifted a dark brow. 'That was quick. Are you sure that you've given it enough time?'

She nodded. 'I'm sure.'

He looked at her doubtfully. 'What decision did you come to?'

'I'll let you know on Monday,' she said. She pulled in a deep breath. 'I have a few things to do right now, so I prefer not to stay around here. I need to start tidying up my life and putting a few plans into action.'

His expression was not what she expected. He looked concerned, a little edgy, as though he was uneasy about exactly what she might have come up with. Perhaps he was worried that she might have made up her mind to stay on in A and E. He might be thinking that her success in helping Jenny and Tom had given her a false sense of security.

'I must go,' she said, and she started to hurry away. She had made her decision, it was true enough, and it was the events of the afternoon that had brought things home to her.

Mark called after her, but she took no notice. She didn't want to stand here and talk to him about it just now. She needed to clear a few things in her head first.

It was all about finding courage and strength of mind, and she had to face her demons once and for all.

She went up to the intensive care unit and enquired after the asthmatic mother and her newborn infant.

'The baby is doing well,' the nurse said. 'He

was resuscitated very quickly, and he's responding much better than we expected. His heart rate and respiration are both good, and he's moving actively. We're pleased with him.'

'What about the mother?'

'We're happy with her progress, too. We're keeping her intubated, but hopefully we'll be able to withdraw the tube some time tomorrow. She'll stay on the heart monitor for now, but that's mostly as a precaution. Once we have her condition fully stabilised, we'll send her over to the maternity unit.'

'That's good to hear,' Sarah said, a warm feeling spreading through her. 'I'm relieved that they're both improving.'

'It must have been a worrying time for you,' the nurse said. 'You hardly ever see these sorts of cases. You must have been really anxious for both of them.'

'I was, but I feel better now. Thanks.'

Sarah left the unit and headed home. She wanted to know how her father and Jamie had fared during the day, and she knew that her father would want to know whether she had managed to sort out her problems.

On Monday morning she walked into A and E, and Mark called her into his office straight away. She frowned. 'I was just going to help out with the people who were injured in the early morning road traffic accident,' she told him.

'We already have staff covering that,' he said curtly. 'If they need help, they'll call us. I'd like a word with you now, if you will.'

Sarah nodded. He was being very formal with her, and it bothered her a little. She had hoped for a more receptive meeting with him, but this didn't bode very well at all. She glanced around and saw that Jonathan was watching her, looking a trifle anxious. Perhaps he had heard some of the rumours going around, and was expecting her to hear bad news.

She followed Mark into his room, and he wasted no time in getting to the point. He stood in front of his desk, leaning back against it, his hands cupping the edge, his long legs thrust out in front of him and crossed at the ankle. He was far too good-looking for her peace of mind, she thought resentfully. Why did she have to be so aware of him at a time like this?

'You said on Saturday that you had managed to think things through. Are you still happy with the decision you made?'

'Yes, I am.'

'Well?'

She straightened her shoulders. 'I realise that you might not like this,' she began, 'but I've decided that I want to stay on. When my contract comes to an end, I'm going to apply for the permanent position in A and E.'

He stared at her. 'Let me get this straight. You want to stay on as an emergency doctor—is that right?'

'That's what I said.' She pressed her lips together momentarily. 'The thing is, although you made it fairly plain to me that you think I'm not up to it, I've come to the conclusion that I was wrong to have so many doubts.'

His brows met in a dark line, but she pushed on, regardless. 'No one can work in A and E and know that they are never going to make a mistake. Everyone must feel a degree of uncertainty, especially to begin with—when you're just starting out, or if you've only had a few months' experience. I've had almost a year in the department, and I can't expect to be an expert. Confidence will come with time. I was wrong to think that I'm no good because I can't always save my patients.'

'I see…I think.' He studied her. 'So, all of a sudden, you're feeling much more self-assured, and you're ready to go back into the fray?' His mouth made a wry twist. 'Forgive me, but I can't help wondering how this miraculous conversion came about.'

She winced. 'It was Jenny and her little boy—the one who nearly went into the duck-pond—who made me realise where I was going wrong. You set out to do good, but you can't always get the best result because quite often you start off with bad odds, and then you can only do your very best to put matters right.' She looked up at him and saw that there was a quizzical expression in his eyes. Perhaps she wasn't making herself clear.

She said, 'The little boy was hurtling towards the pond, and his mother wanted to save him and prevent him from coming to any harm. She couldn't save him because the odds were against her, and so she did the next best thing. She made sure that, one way or another, he was going to survive. It wasn't the best of outcomes because he banged his head, but at least he didn't drown, and at least he didn't go crashing down onto the bottom of the concrete pond.'

Mark moved away from the desk. 'So you're saying that a doctor can only do his or her best in the circumstances? You're saying that there is sometimes a chance that the patient might die or suffer the consequences of his illness or accident, but the doctor does his or her best, and tries to get the most satisfactory outcome possible?'

She swallowed. She wasn't entirely sure that he agreed with her. His manner was slightly

odd, and it wasn't at all what she was used to.
'That's what I'm saying.'

He began to smile and now it was her turn to
look at him oddly.

'Why are you smiling?' she asked.

'Because you finally seem to have worked it
out,' he said. He shook his head. 'Well, it's about
time. I thought the penny would never drop.'

'What do you mean?'

He came over to her and put his hands on her
shoulders, his thumbs lightly caressing her.
'How many times have I told you that you did
what you could to help a patient and that, if the
outcome wasn't the best, it wasn't your fault?
You did what you could for Ryan, and it wasn't
your fault that he suffered a haematoma and
went into a coma. There was nothing you could
have done to prevent that, and there was no
way you could have treated it at the roadside.'

He looked down at her, and his hands were
stroking the length of her arms, filling her with
warmth, sending little spirals of sensation to
spark along all her nerve endings.

'You thought you had made a mistake when you were about to discharge the man with the tumour in his salivary gland. How were you supposed to know that it was a tumour? I guessed, because I have years of experience behind me, but you did the right thing anyway. You sent him for an urgent consultation. That's what any other doctor would have done.'

She frowned. Despite the wonderful feelings that were flowing through her because of the way he was touching her, the way his hands were caressing her, she had to remind herself that he was the one who had told her that she was not up to it, that she wasn't cut out to be an emergency doctor. Bewildered, she said, 'Why did you tell me that I was no good at my job?'

'I couldn't see any other way to make you stop and think. I tried telling you that you weren't to blame when things went wrong, but you didn't believe me, and in the end I decided that shock tactics were called for.' He drew her to him, holding her close. 'I wanted you to go away and work it out for yourself.'

Her mouth made a crooked slant. 'I think your strategy worked. I couldn't believe that you were actually telling me that I was no good. I was stunned to have you agree with me. It wasn't a very nice experience, and it isn't one that I would ever want to repeat.' She had been falling in love with him, and it had hurt that he was sending her out into the cold. Now that she was in his arms again, it was like coming home.

He made a wry face. 'I can echo that. I was scared out of my wits that you'd come back and tell me that you were off to go and work in Paediatrics, or that you would take me up on the research programme.'

He lifted his hand and ran his thumb gently over her cheek. 'I was so worried that I'd gone too far that I almost went looking for you to tell you that I didn't mean it.'

'You know,' she said softly, 'I'm glad that I was able to find out for myself. When I saw what happened with Jenny and the little boy, it came to me that you have to have faith in yourself, and you can only do your very best. You can't do any more than that.'

He lowered his head and kissed her full on the mouth. 'You can't know how relieved I am,' hc said. 'I thought I'd blown it. I'm so glad to know that I didn't.'

There was a knock at the door, and they sprang apart as Jonathan put his head around it and looked at them. 'We've more patients coming in,' he said. 'We need everybody we can get to help out.'

'We're on our way,' Mark murmured.

Sarah followed him to the door, and then went with Jonathan to prepare for the patients. She was feeling a little shaky after the abrupt end to her meeting with Mark. She hadn't expected such warmth and closeness, and she had been dazed to find that he cared enough to make her discover the truth.

Now that she was back in the real world, though, she realised that he might simply have been trying to make her feel better about herself. It didn't mean that he felt for her in the same way that she had grown to care for him. She loved him, but it was probably a fruitless love.

She went with Jonathan to the ambulance bay to receive the patients. He said, 'You're not going to leave us, are you?'

'What makes you think that I would be leaving?'

'It was just something that Mark said. He mentioned that you were interested in working in Paediatrics. He said you'd been thinking about it, but he thought we would be losing a good doctor if you went. I agree with him. You've taught me so much, and I was hoping that you would stay. You're always so cool and level-headed, and you're an inspiration to me.'

Sarah sent him a quick glance. 'Thanks, but you shouldn't think that I have all the answers. It might appear that way to you, but it can be difficult, trying to think quickly, trying to think on your feet.'

He nodded. 'I said that to Mark, and he said that sometimes we need to stop and take a moment to think before we act. He said that quick thinking isn't always good, and that sometimes a more measured response is called for.'

Sarah felt a warm glow pass through her. Had he really said that? 'He's probably right. As for Paediatrics, I've decided that I'd really prefer to stay in A and E. If there's a place for me here, that's where I would like to be.'

Jonathan looked pleased. 'I'm really glad to hear that. It means that I'll probably be working alongside you for a while yet. I hope that's all right with you?'

'That's fine by me.' She sent him an answering smile, and then they both concentrated on work as the ambulance pulled in alongside them.

It was late in the afternoon by the time she managed to go along to see Hannah. She went into her sister's room cautiously, unsure of her reception and worried in case the physiotherapy hadn't been going well.

Hannah was standing, supported by a metal frame to the side of her, and she looked up as

Sarah came into the room. 'Look, Sarah,' she said. 'I can take a few steps. Isn't that great?'

'That's wonderful,' Sarah said. 'I'm so happy for you. That is real progress.'

The nurse who had been helping Hannah said, 'I think you should rest now, Hannah. You've done enough for today.' She helped her to sit down in a chair at the side of the bed, and Sarah went to sit alongside her.

'It's good to see you looking so well, Hannah,' she said as the nurse left the room.

'I feel so much better,' Hannah said. She touched Sarah's arm. 'I was awful to you, the other day, wasn't I? For the last few days, in fact. I should never have said those things to you. I don't know why I did—I think it's because I needed somebody to blame, and you were there. It was too easy to strike out at you. You've always been so good at everything you do, whereas I'm the one who's made a mess of my life.'

Hannah looked at Sarah anxiously. 'I suppose it was a chance to hit out, to make myself believe that even you could make a mistake. I know that you didn't. I knew in my heart that you had done everything you could to help Ryan. It was unfair of me, and I'm so sorry.'

Sarah hugged her sister. 'It's all right. I know that you didn't mean it.'

She looked at Hannah and said slowly, 'You know, it isn't true that I never make a mistake. It might seem that way to you, but the truth is I struggle with everything. Over the last few weeks I've come to realise that I've spent my life trying to live up to people's expectations of me. Dad's always assumed that I'll never put a foot wrong, and it's been really difficult to live up to that. I've always felt guilty. I've never been truly confident, and I didn't know how to tell him that until recently.'

Hannah shook her head. 'I didn't realise what you were going through,' she said softly. 'I've often thought that I messed things up and I felt unsure of myself, and I wished that Mum was alive so that I could tell her all my troubles. Perhaps if you had been able to confide in her, you would have felt stronger.'

'I think you're right. I spoke to Dad about it last night, and he thinks we should all talk more about our troubles, and bring things out into the open. You've been struggling because of your worries about Ryan, before the accident and since, but perhaps between us we can work something out.'

Hannah nodded. 'Yes. I think that would help. If he comes through this, I want to persuade him to go ahead with some sort of counselling. Before the accident, just before the accident, he said that he thought the drinking was in part to do with his working away so much. He felt isolated, and because he had been away so long, he never felt that he had a place where he really belonged.' She grimaced. 'That sounds odd, but I think I know what he meant. I think he meant that he didn't fit in, and I need to show him that he has a home with Jamie and me.' She smiled. 'He said that we should marry.'

Sarah's mouth curved. 'I hope it works out for you. You don't have to rush into anything, though. Take your time, and work things out first.'

They talked for a while longer, and then Sarah prepared to leave. 'I should get back to work,' she said. 'I've another hour to do before my shift ends. I'll kiss Jamie for you, and I'll bring him to see you tomorrow.'

The hour passed quickly enough, but when Sarah was getting ready to go home Mark came and found her. 'I wondered if I could come by your father's house tonight and drop something off?' he said. 'It's to do with work. Would that be all right, or do you have plans for this evening?'

Sarah couldn't imagine what he wanted to bring with him that was to do with work, unless it was some files that he needed to go over with her. It was an unusual request, but she had told him that she wanted to stay on in A and E, and perhaps it was to do with that.

She said, 'I was actually planning on going to the cottage this evening. Jamie is having a sleepover at a friend's house, and I thought I'd take the opportunity to go and sort a few things out at my place. Since Hannah has been in hospital, I've hardly been back there. It's been easier to stay with Jamie and Kingston at my dad's house. You could come over to me there, if you like.'

'That suits me. Shall we say around eight o'clock?'

'That'll be fine.'

She went home and made preparations for Jamie to go to stay with his friend. 'Do you want to take some toys with you, Jamie?' she asked.

He nodded, and she said, 'You'd better go and sort them out, then, and I'll put them in a bag for you.'

'All right.' He jumped down from the sofa, where he had been playing with his toy soldiers, and hopped and skipped to the door, singing a little tune to himself as he went.

Sarah watched him. Then she turned to her father, who had just come in from the garden, and said with a smile, 'He's a happy little soul today, isn't he? Do you think it's because he is going to stay with Robert?'

'Could be,' her father said, 'but, then, it might be because he went to see his dad at the hospital. I took him there after I finished my afternoon surgery.'

'I remember you said that you might do that, if you had the time. Did the visit go well?'

Her father smiled. 'It went remarkably well, actually. Jamie had been chatting away the whole time, without expecting any response from his dad, and then he decided to tell him about the clay pot he had made for him. The thing is, Ryan suddenly said, "I know."'

Sarah stared at him. 'You're joking?'

Her father shook his head. 'I'm not.'

Jamie bounced back into the room just then. 'I didn't believe Daddy,' he said. 'So I said to him, "All right, then, what colour is it?"' He chuckled. 'Daddy said, "Sunshine yellow."'

Jamie waved his hands in the air, palms uppermost, as though he was asking a question. 'How could he know that? And Daddy didn't even sit up,' he exclaimed. 'Grandad says that's really good, though. He says Daddy's going to get better, like Mummy.'

Sarah was open-mouthed. She looked from

Jamie to her father. 'That is such good news. That's wonderful.'

Jamie skipped out of the room once more, and she heard him banging up the stairs to his room. 'No wonder he's so cheerful,' she said.

'Things are looking up,' her father agreed. He glanced at her as she folded Jamie's pyjamas and put them into a little overnight case. 'Did you say that you were going to your cottage tonight? Only I thought I might go and visit some friends later on, seeing that Jamie is going to be away for the night. We were planning to play cards. I'll probably be back quite late, but I'll see that Kingston's settled down before I leave.'

'That's fine. You go and enjoy yourself. I've one or two things to do back at my place—a good scoot round with the vacuum cleaner, for one thing, and a bit of dusting.'

She didn't mention that Mark would be paying her a visit. She wasn't at all sure what that was all about. Even so, she couldn't quell the little bubble of excitement that started up in her. He had wanted her to have faith in herself, and he had held her close and that had to be good.

By the time eight o'clock came around she had finished tidying up at the cottage, and she was pleased that she had put everything in good order. Then the doubts began to creep in.

Mark was so used to his parents' grand house, and his own place was perfection itself—what on earth had she been thinking of when she had invited him to this little rabbit hutch?

The doorbell rang, and she hurriedly checked her hair in the mirror and smoothed down imaginary creases in her skirt. Her hair was wild as usual, but it was too late to do anything more with it. She was nervous, wanting to see him yet afraid because she was yearning for something that was probably impossible. She worked with him, that was all. What made her think that his kisses meant anything more than a sweet flirtation?

He looked wonderful, in casual chinos and a pale-coloured linen shirt. He was carrying a box, a fairly large box, and she frowned, wondering how many files it held. Did he really expect to work this evening? A frisson of disappointment washed through her.

'I've made some coffee,' she said, showing him into the sitting room. 'I thought it would be more comfortable in here. Do you want to sit down?' She waved a hand towards the sofa, and hoped that her nervousness didn't show. She didn't know why she was so keyed up.

'Thanks,' he said. 'Come and sit down next to me.' He reached for her and tugged her down beside him. 'I brought you something.' He handed her the box. 'Open it.'

Puzzled, she looked from him to the box. 'Is this the work that you were talking about?' She hesitated. 'Do we have to start work straight away?'

He gave a crooked smile. 'I think I might have misled you just a little,' he said. 'This is sort of to do with work. Open it, and let me know what you think.'

She pulled at the thin ribbon that tied up the

box, and he helped her when she struggled to remove it. His fingers brushed hers, and the spark of contact burned a path along the full length of her arm and made her glance at him fleetingly. Heat ran along her cheekbones.

Finally, she managed to lift the cover off the box, and she saw layers of tissue paper. 'What is it?' she asked. Cautiously, she pulled back the layers, and there, nestled among the tissue, was the most beautiful dress that she had ever seen. It was made of a soft fabric, shot through with strands that glistened faintly, and there were thin little straps and a skirt that ended with a flourish of filmy layers of the same beautiful fabric. She looked up at him, her eyes widening. 'I don't understand,' she said. 'Why have you bought this for me?'

'I wanted to say that I was sorry for putting you through all that trauma this last weekend. I wanted to make up for the fact that you lost your own lovely dress when you were saving the little girl. I wanted to give you this before

now, but I wasn't sure how you would react.'
He looked at her searchingly. 'Do you like it?'

'It's beautiful,' she said. She looked into his
eyes. 'You didn't have to do this, you
know…but I think it's lovely, the most beautiful dress I've ever seen. Thank you.'

He gently took it from her and laid it over the
arm of the sofa. He pushed the box away, and
then he took hold of her hands in his and he
said, 'I know that this is probably the wrong
time—your sister is ill, and you have the worry
of looking after little Jamie—but I want you to
know—I need you to know—that I love you.
I've loved you for a long, long time.'

She blinked. 'Do you mean it?' She held her
breath, afraid that this was all a dream. 'Did I
imagine what you said?'

'I mean it. I love you. I was so afraid that I
might lose you. It was bad enough that I
thought you might go to Owen, but when
I thought that I might have pushed you away, I
was in a terrible state. I really thought I had
gone too far. It's made me realise that I need to

tell you exactly how I feel about you, Sarah. I love you. Is there just a chance that you might feel the same way about me?'

She reached up and touched his face with her fingertips. 'I didn't believe that this could happen,' she whispered. 'I thought that our lives were so far apart that we could never be together.' She frowned. 'It was over between me and Owen a long, long time ago. You must believe that. There was never a possibility that I would be going to him.'

She ran her fingers lightly over his cheekbones, along the length of his jaw, exploring the contours of his face as though she would memorise them. 'I do love you, Mark, but I don't think love can work for you and me. My life is so different to yours. You've been used to so much wealth, your background is so different to mine—and your parents must think I'm a terrible person after what happened at their house. It would never work out between us, would it?'

He laughed. 'My parents think you're adorable,' he said. 'They even have a soft spot for Kingston, despite what he did to the flower-beds.' He kissed her, a soft, coaxing kiss that made her want to snuggle up and lose herself in him. 'We're just a normal family, you know. We may be privileged in that we have money and all the comforts that it brings, but we're ordinary human beings and we want the same things as everyone else, to be able to love and care for our own.'

He drew her to him and kissed her once more, tenderly exploring the softness of her lips. 'I want to share my life with you,' he murmured huskily. 'I don't want to go through all the uncertainty and heartache any longer. It's killing me.'

He looked into her eyes. 'Will you marry me, Sarah? Will you be my wife?'

'I will,' she whispered. She pulled in a long, shaky breath. 'I'll love you for ever.'

He wrapped his arms around her and kissed her, making her senses swirl and driving every thought from her head. 'You've just made me the happiest man on earth,' he said huskily. He smiled. 'I think a summer wedding would be good, don't you? Shall we say around two months from now?'

'That sounds good to me,' she murmured, her body meshing with his, her soft lips parting for his kiss.

MEDICAL ROMANCE™

Large Print

Titles for the next six months…

September

HIS SECRET LOVE-CHILD	Marion Lennox
HER HONOURABLE PLAYBOY	Kate Hardy
THE SURGEON'S PREGNANCY SURPRISE	
	Laura MacDonald
IN HIS LOVING CARE	Jennifer Taylor
HIGH-ALTITUDE DOCTOR	Sarah Morgan
A FRENCH DOCTOR AT ABBEYFIELDS	Abigail Gordon

October

THE DOCTOR'S UNEXPECTED PROPOSAL	
	Alison Roberts
THE DOCTOR'S SURPRISE BRIDE	Fiona McArthur
A KNIGHT TO HOLD ON TO	Lucy Clark
HER BOSS AND PROTECTOR	Joanna Neil
THE SURGEON'S CONVENIENT FIANCÉE	Rebecca Lang
THE SURGEON'S MARRIAGE RESCUE	Leah Martyn

November

HIS HONOURABLE SURGEON	Kate Hardy
PREGNANT WITH HIS CHILD	Lilian Darcy
THE CONSULTANT'S ADOPTED SON	Jennifer Taylor
HER LONGED-FOR FAMILY	Josie Metcalfe
MISSION: MOUNTAIN RESCUE	Amy Andrews
THE GOOD FATHER	Maggie Kingsley

MILLS & BOON®

Live the emotion

0806 LP 2P P1 Medical

MEDICAL ROMANCE™

Large Print

MILLS & BOON®

Live the emotion

0806 LP 2P P2 Medical